CW00823436

FLYNN'S FOLLY

Following the death of her father in a mysterious road accident, Jessica returns to The Folly, her home on Exmoor, to find the house neglected and a once-thriving business on the verge of collapse. Determined not to lose her home, she sets out to save The Folly. But who can she turn to for help? And which man can she trust? The family friend she has known all her life — or the stranger who threatens her very livelihood?

GAIL CRANE

◆

FLYNN'S FOLLY

Complete and Unabridged

LINFORD
Leicester

First published in Great Britain in 2021

First Linford Edition
published 2022

*A catalogue record for this book is available
from the British Library.*

ISBN 978–1–4448–4921–9

Published by
Ulverscroft Limited
Anstey, Leicestershire

Printed and bound in Great Britain by
TJ Books Ltd., Padstow, Cornwall

This book is printed on acid-free paper

After the Funeral

It isn't just the cold making me shiver as I stand by my father's grave in the tiny hillside cemetery on Exmoor. It's that same question I've been asking myself over and over since I came back from Australia.

What happened to cause the accident that killed him?

Matthew Hall, the vicar, is waiting for people to make their way to the grave from the church and I'm pleased to see most of Larkcombe village has come to say goodbye to Dad. Not that I'm surprised. He was well-liked.

Next to me, Aunt Isobel is rubbing her hands to keep warm. She's actually my great-aunt, Grandpa's older sister, though you'd never think so to look at her.

She's still tall, slim and black-haired, like all the Flynns, and hates to be called 'Aunt', saying it makes her feel old. Yet she must be well into her eighties.

1

'I wish the man would get on with it before we all die of cold,' she grumbles.

Never the most tactful of people, she believes in saying what she means.

In this instance, I agree with her. I'm longing to get home where I can give way to grief and say my own private goodbye to Dad.

I wipe away a tear with my gloved hand.

Giles, standing next to me, takes my other hand.

'You OK, Jessica?'

I nod.

'Mm, thanks.'

Despite the occasion, it's good to be back here after almost two years away.

Is there any more beautiful place than this to end one's days? Halfway up a hill, with the church above and the valley below, and across the vale the moor's purple peaks.

The only signs of habitation are a few scattered cottages and farms. All is peace and quiet.

There are some faces I don't recognise

2

but most are familiar to me.

I'm intrigued by one man standing apart from the rest. I don't recognise him as being from the village, though of course there will have been changes since I left.

There's something about his appearance — his expensive suit, as if he's come from a board meeting, and the way he's keeping his distance — that makes me uneasy.

At last, Matthew begins. As he speaks the emotive words of the funeral service my throat constricts and I fight to hold back the tears.

Giles passes me his handkerchief and as Matthew begins the ashes-to-ashes bit and the coffin is lowered slowly into the grave I can no longer hold back the sobs.

As soon as it's over, Isobel steers me to the waiting car.

'Come along, let's get home. I don't know about you, but I need a stiff drink.'

People begin filing out of the cemetery, pausing to smile or shake my hand or kiss my cheek.

Again I notice the stranger. He pauses, as if wondering whether to come over, then moves away without speaking.

I rather expected Giles to come with us but he apologises and makes his excuses, saying he has to meet someone.

'I'll be along later,' he tells me, 'if I can get away.'

Isobel and I settle into the limousine and I lean against the headrest and close my eyes with a sigh of relief as the car takes us back to Larkcombe and the Folly.

'Thank goodness that's over. I wonder how many will come back to the house.'

Isobel huffs.

'Most of the village, I expect. You know how they are. Any excuse for a get-together and gossip.'

'Isobel!' I can't help a smile, though, because she's right. 'It's natural Dad's friends want to remember him.'

'Well, I'm glad that Giles fellow isn't coming. I don't like him and I've never understood what your father saw in him.'

Giles is younger than Dad, in fact not

much older than me, but for some reason they got on well. Probably because they were in similar businesses, though Giles's place is very different to the Folly.

'He's been good to me since I got back,' I tell her. 'He seems keen to help any way he can.'

'You watch him, my girl. Nobody does anything without a reason.'

I pat her hand affectionately.

'You're an old cynic. But don't worry, I have every intention of being extremely careful.'

'I should hope so.'

We sit in silence for a few minutes and I think again about the way Dad died. Maybe I'm imagining things but I wonder what Isobel thinks about it.

'Isobel, this might sound silly but don't you think there's something odd about the accident? I mean, why would a perfectly fit man in the prime of life swerve off a quiet country road for no apparent reason?'

She looks at me, surprised.

'Why would you think it odd?'

'Well, according to reports, there was no traffic and no-one else was involved. The weather was fine and the visibility good.

'The road at that point is straight and Dad knew it like the back of his hand, yet he somehow managed to drive off the road and straight into a tree.'

'I imagine there could be any number of reasons. A deer on the road. A momentary lapse of concentration. Perhaps he was on the phone.'

'No. He was a good, careful driver and he would never have done anything stupid. And there was nothing to suggest any animal being involved.'

'The police seem satisfied it was an accident, Jessica.'

'I know, and there's nothing to suggest otherwise, so, as far as anyone else is concerned, the case is closed. But I'm sure there's more to it.'

We are approaching Larkcombe village.

'Will you stay in the house, Isobel?' I ask. 'Or would you prefer somewhere else?'

Isobel has never liked the Folly and

left many years ago when Mum and Dad started talking about taking paying guests, saying there was no way she was going to share her home with strangers.

As it happened, Mum died before they did anything about it, but by then Isobel was comfortably settled elsewhere.

'I could ask Sue James if she has room at Primrose Cottage,' I suggest, thinking she might prefer the pretty thatched cottage in the village.

Isobel grunts.

'The Folly will do fine. I'm assuming there are no guests at the moment?'

'Just you and me,' I assure her.

'That's how it should be. Just family.'

Just family would be lovely, I think, but taking in guests is our only way of making a living and being able to keep our home.

That's another thing that bothers me. When I left for Australia business was good, but since coming home I've been struck by how neglected the house looks.

And there are no bookings. Why?

Dad seems to have completely let

things go and that wasn't like him. It's something else that doesn't feel right.

We turn into the lane that runs up the combe to the house. As we make our way along the winding drive, I think whoever named it the Folly was spot on.

The house was built in the days when people had servants and it is far too big for a single family in the 21st century. Who needs eight bedrooms these days?

Molly, who for years has come from the village to clean and generally help Dad with running the house, stepped in to help soon after Mum died and I doubt we would have managed without her.

The grounds need an army of gardeners to keep them in check and although Molly's husband, Mike, does his best, he's fighting a losing battle.

For all its faults, it's my home and I love it, though it's hard to imagine it without Dad. I can't believe I'll never see him again.

As Isobel predicted, most people have come back to the house and are congregating in the big hall. When my grandparents were alive this room was the scene of many family celebrations.

It holds a mish-mash of comfy sofas and easy chairs arranged around the huge fireplace, with faded rugs scattered over bare oak floorboards.

Tall windows look out over a sweep of lawn towards the sea in the distance. As a child I'd sit, curled up, on one of the broad window-seats, immersed in a book or deep in thought.

Molly comes over and hands me a glass of wine. She's laid out an array of refreshments and drinks on the huge refectory table at the end of the room opposite the fireplace.

She gives me a hug.

'How are you? What a lovely service.'

'Yes, it was. I'm fine, thank you.'

'Good. You'll be glad when it's all over and you can be on your own for a while. I've put out the food and drinks.'

She looks around the room at the increasing numbers.

'I just hope I've done enough.'

'I'm sure you have. It's wonderful, Molly.'

9

'Sam would be pleased to see all these people here, don't you think?'

'I think he'd be surprised to know how much people think of him.'

Dad was a modest man and he would be touched that so many have come.

Molly nods.

'Such a lovely man. Well, I'll let you be but I'll be here to clear up afterwards.'

She turns, but not before I notice the tears in her eyes. She will miss him, too.

I should make the effort to mingle. I wonder if the stranger at the cemetery is here, but there's no sign of him. I push him from my mind as people come up to offer their condolences.

Isobel has vanished, probably to Grandpa's old sitting-room at the back of the house. He, like Isobel, never enjoyed company and spent many hours in that room with his books and pipe, hiding from his gregarious wife's many friends and visitors.

Clare, my old schoolfriend and Dad's part-time bookkeeper, comes over.

'You look lost,' she says, putting a

hand on my arm. 'Why don't you come and sit down for a while?'

I smile at her.

'I do feel a bit washed out.'

'Hardly surprising after all you've been through. Let's go somewhere quiet.'

I let her take me through to the kitchen where she sits me down at the table and pours two large glasses of Chardonnay.

'Here, drink this.'

'I've had one already,' I protest.'I'll get tipsy.'

'Then have another. It will do you good, help you unwind.'

I take the glass and drink, savouring the fruity taste of the wine and the slightly fuzzy feeling it's giving me. I'm definitely beginning to feel more relaxed.

I lean back in my chair and sigh.

'What will I do without Dad, Clare?'

'You'll carry on, that's what you'll do. You'll manage. And I'll be here to help.'

I smile at her.

'I know. But we had such plans! I'm not sure I can do it on my own.'

'Of course you can. I know you well

enough to know you'll find a way. At the moment you're down, naturally.

'You'll feel better when the initial shock has worn off.'

'Perhaps you're right.'

I'm not so sure, but right now all I'm bothered about is getting through the rest of today.

'I know I'm right. You're a fighter, always have been, and I can't see you giving up now. You owe it to yourself and to Sam to keep going.'

'I'm glad you have such faith in me.'

I swallow the last of the wine, remembering all the work Dad and I put into the Folly.

I think again of the man at the funeral.

'Clare, did you notice that man at the cemetery? The one in the suit, standing apart from the others?'

'There were several in suits.'

'Not like this one. I'm pretty sure he wasn't a local and I'm certain I've never seen him before.'

She shakes her head.

'Sorry, I don't remember anyone in

particular.'

'He looked so out of place. There's something about him that bothers me and I can't stop thinking about him.'

'You're just feeling the stress of the past few days. I'm sure there is nothing to worry about.'

'I wish Giles was here. He might know who he is.'

'Stop worrying, Jess. Sam had friends all over the place.'

'You're right. I'm probably over-reacting.'

I stand up, feeling my head reel slightly from the effects of the wine.

'I should get back to the hall before everyone leaves . . . and while I can still stand!'

'Are you feeling better now?'

'Wobbly but better. Thanks, Clare. See you later.'

★ ★ ★

I go to bed that night, mulling over all that has happened.

Dad was all the family I had apart from Isobel. It was always just the two of us after cancer took Mum soon after my fifteenth birthday.

Dad and I comforted and supported each other through the days and months that followed and slowly we picked up the broken strands of our lives.

We threw ourselves into making a living from the Folly by turning it into a B&B.

The house had been built by my several times-great-grandfather, Jonas, on Larkcombe Ridge, halfway up an Exmoor combe overlooking the sea.

It has been our family home for more than 150 years.

After school I did whatever I could to help Dad, often earning black looks and lines from teachers the following day for not completing homework.

But the Folly was, and still is, my passion. Who cared about school? Certainly not me.

The long holidays were heaven. Dad built and repaired while I painted and cleaned.

We ate sandwiches while sitting on the grassy slope we later coaxed into being a lawn, with the house at our backs and the wide expanse of Larkcombe Bay in front of us.

'We'll make a go of this, won't we, Jessie, love?' Dad said the day before we welcomed our first guests.

'You bet,' I told him. 'We'll have the best B&B in the whole of Exmoor.'

Over the next few years, we went from strength to strength. Then I had a call from an old schoolfriend, Helen, about a temporary job in Australia, working on a cattle station.

'You have to come, Jess. Just think of it — two years out here on the station! It'll be hard work but you'll love it.'

I was worried about leaving Dad to cope on his own, but he was determined I should go.

'I'll be fine,' he assured me. 'I have Molly and Clare and it's the chance of a lifetime for you. Go and enjoy yourself.

'Just mind you come home again.'

'Try to keep me away!' I'd replied.

So, now I'm home, but what I've seen since I arrived has really shocked me, and I wonder what on earth has been going on while I've been gone.

An Unwelcome Visitor

The next morning I'm finishing breakfast when Clare arrives. She lets herself
in as I'm putting the used dishes in the
dishwasher.

I'm about to head to the office when
the bell in reception pings.

There's a man standing at the desk
with his back to me. I see impeccably
styled dark hair cut to just above his collar, a pair of broad shoulders, and long
legs encased in slimline trousers.

From the way his suit hangs on his tall
frame it's clear it hasn't been bought off
the peg. It shrieks quality and money.

He can't be here to book a room. The
guests the Folly usually attracts are the
walkingboots-and-backpack brigade and
this man is far too smartly dressed to be
one of those.

I wonder why he isn't at the Mermaid
along with the Savile Row and Rolex set.

He turns and I catch my breath. It's
the man from the funeral.

Despite my uneasiness, my stomach gives a little flip. I guess he's probably early thirties, and much too attractive. As he smiles at me his eyes crinkle at the corners. They're brown, the colour of ripe chestnuts.

I realise I'm staring and pull myself together and go into professional mode.

'Good morning. Can I help you?'

'I'm looking for Jessica Flynn.'

'That's me.'

His handshake is firm and confident.

'I'm Max Corrigan.' His voice is as rich and sexy as his eyes.

I nod.

'You were at the funeral. But you didn't come back to the house afterwards.'

'I didn't want to intrude.'

'Did you know my father?'

'Yes, though not well — in a business capacity mainly. My father and he were friends. I was sorry to hear about the accident. It must have been a shock.'

The look of sympathy on his face is almost my undoing. For some ridiculous reason, I have an urge to put my head on his shoulder and sob into that expensive suit.

How good it would feel to have a man put his arms round me and soothe away the anger and hurt.

I straighten my shoulders and manage to find a smile from somewhere.

'It was, thank you. How can I help you?'

Since he hadn't known Dad well, I wonder why he's come to see me.

'I don't know how much your father explained to you about our arrangement,' he says, 'but I'm afraid there are important matters we need to discuss.'

Something in his voice tells me I'm not going to like what he has to say.

'What sort of matters?' I struggle to keep my voice steady.

'I'm sorry,' he says, 'this is insensitive of me. It must be painful for you and our business can wait another day or so.

'Why don't I come back another time?'

It's tempting to say yes, but then I'll be wondering what this is all about and that isn't going to help my already sleepless nights. I shake my head.

'No, it's all right. I have time. Let's go into the office.'

'Are you sure?'

'Perfectly. Can I get you some tea or coffee?'

He gives me that smile again. He has a small scar under his left eye. Far from detracting from his good looks, the little imperfection makes him even more attractive.

How can I even be thinking that, when I fear he brings bad news?

'Coffee would be lovely. Thank you.'

I show him into the office and go to the kitchen. Luckily there is enough for two cups left in the pot.

When I get back, he's browsing our brochures. I put the tray down on the desk.

'Milk or sugar?'

'Neither, thanks.'

I take my own cup and sit opposite him at the desk. I nod towards the brochures.

'That's one of the things Dad was

planning to have redesigned before he . . .' I'm still finding it difficult to actually say the word.

'They could certainly do with updating. But that's one of the things we can look at together. I assume you'll be taking over from your father?'

'Naturally.'

I'm taken aback by the question and his comment about doing things together.

'This is my home. And my livelihood now.'

'Of course,' he says. 'I understand that.'

'Then perhaps we could get to the point, Mr Corrigan. You say you have matters to discuss. Please tell me what they are.'

'Why don't you call me Max?'

There's that smile again but this time I'm not falling for it.

'After all,' he continues, 'we're going to see a lot of each other from now on, so 'Mr' is a bit formal, don't you think?'

There's something here I'm missing.

'I'm sorry, I don't understand. Will

you please explain?'

'Well, if we are going to be working together it will be easier to meet occasionally. Phones and internet are all very well but nothing beats sitting down and talking face to face.

'I have other business interests, of course, so won't be able to spend more than, say, two days a month here.'

'Hold on a minute, Mr Corrigan!'

'Max.'

I ignore the interruption.

'Can we just rewind and start from the beginning? Because I don't have the foggiest idea what you're talking about.'

He looks as puzzled as I am.

'Forgive me. I assumed Sam would have explained all this to you.'

'Explained what?'

He leans back in his chair and frowns.

'You really don't have any idea what this is about, do you?'

He looks uncomfortable.

'I'm sorry, Jessica, but in that case I think what I have to say may come as a shock. I can't imagine why Sam hasn't told you.'

'I've been away in Australia, so maybe he was waiting until I came home.'

I can't think of any other reason he wouldn't have told me about something as important as this clearly is.

'It still seems odd he didn't mention anything at all. You must have communicated somehow.'

'Of course we did. E-mail, Skype. But he never said anything about you.'

That reminds me that I only have this man's word for what he's telling me.

'Can you give me one good reason, Mr Corrigan, why I should believe you?'

He takes a document from his briefcase and passes it to me.

'About a month ago, Sam set up a power of attorney authorising me to help with his financial affairs. This is a copy of that agreement.'

My insides churn as I read the document. He watches patiently as I turn the pages.

'I've never seen this before.'

'Surely Sam's copy is with his papers?

Hasn't his solicitor told you about it?'

I shake my head.

'My solicitor has said nothing. This is the first I've heard of it.' I swallow. 'Why on earth would my father give you power of attorney?'

I put the document down on the desk. Can this be true? I'm no legal expert but it does appear to be genuine.

But why haven't I found Dad's copy amongst his things? He must surely have had one.

More to the point, why hadn't Dad said anything to me? This is my home, for heaven's sake. I helped Dad build the B&B business. How could he give control of it to a complete stranger?

I feel a sudden surge of anger. It isn't fair, and I'm damned if I'm going to let this Corrigan fellow get away with it. I'll find a way out of it somehow.

I have a thought.

'Hold on a minute. Wouldn't Dad's death invalidate a power of attorney?'

'You're right, it does. But that's not the whole story. Sam wouldn't give me

24

details, but it seems he made some bad decisions. He'd been encouraged to invest in some get-rich-quick project, got in deeper than he intended and lost a lot of money.

'He also ended up owing money. So that he could pay his debts, I arranged a loan for him in return for a share in the business.'

'Why would you do that?'

'As I say, my father and he were friends. They go back a long way and my father asked for my help.

'So you see, I have money invested in this business, hence my need to be a part of getting it back on its feet again. You should have a copy of the loan agreement among your father's papers.'

This is like a bad dream! Whatever has Dad been up to? Everything I'm hearing is completely out of character for him.

He was always so careful with money and he would never have done something like this Max Corrigan is suggesting.

I don't believe it. What if he's making it up? He could be a conman, after all.

I push my chair back and stand up.

'That is not true. Dad would not do something like that.'

'I know it must be difficult for you, but I'm afraid he did.'

'You're wrong. That's not like Dad at all. There has to be some mistake. Either that or you are lying to me.'

Adrenaline is pumping through me. My head's pounding and I can't begin to think what the implications of all this might be.

Max stands and picks up his briefcase.

'Jessica, this has clearly been a shock for you and I'm sorry, I didn't mean it to be. I naturally assumed you knew.

'I can't tell why Sam would want to keep anything from you but I think you need time to collect your thoughts. Perhaps we should leave it for a while and talk again in a day or two.'

He's right, I do need time to think, but right now I just want him gone.

I walk with him to the hall. He turns at the door and takes my hand.

'I really am sorry you had to find out

like this, Jessica. I'll give you a call soon to arrange another meeting.'

I watch him walk across the car park towards a black Mercedes convertible.

As he drives away, I wonder why this man wants to waste time getting involved with a struggling B&B.

★ ★ ★

I head for the kitchen, thoroughly shaken by Max Corrigan's visit. Clare is replenishing the coffee-maker and turns as I go in.

'My word, Jess, what's up? You look as though you've lost a pound and found a penny.'

'More than a pound, and I'm not sure I've even found a penny.'

I pull out a chair and collapse on to it, leaning my elbows on the table and resting my pounding head in my hands.

'Brew enough for two, will you? And make it good and strong.'

'My, this sounds serious.'

She flicks the switch, sets the coffee

bubbling, and reaches for the biscuit tin.

She sits down opposite me and pushes the open tin across the table.

'Serious enough for some choccy comfort?'

Why not? What will a few extra pounds or pimples matter when I'm about to lose everything I love?

I fish for my favourite chocolate-covered orange biscuit and bite into it, wishing it was Max Corrigan I'm crushing to crumbs.

Clare watches me with a worried look. 'OK, tell me about it.'

'I've just had a visitor. Max Corrigan.'

'I saw him.' She grins. 'Sexy!'

'Sexy he might be. He's also trouble.'

I reach for another biscuit then change my mind and slam the lid down with a bang.

'I'll pour the coffee.'

'Stay where you are. I'll get it.'

Clare fills two mugs and carries them to the table. I wrap my hands round mine, feeling the comforting warmth, and try to control the tears that are threatening again.

Clare and I have been friends since we were at playgroup. We went to the same schools and only parted company when I left to study business management at Exeter and she took a bookkeeping course in Taunton.

When Dad offered her the part-time job as bookkeeper it enabled her to go freelance and begin her own business.

'What's wrong?' she asks. 'You know what they say about a trouble shared.'

True, and if there's anyone I can share this problem with, it's her.

'Have you found anything among Dad's papers that looks like a power of attorney?'

She ponders for a moment, then shakes her head.

'I don't think so. But wouldn't anything like that be with his solicitor?'

'I suppose so. He told me to contact him after the funeral to go through everything and I think the sooner I do that the better.'

'Why do you ask?'

'According to Corrigan, Dad gave him

power of attorney to deal with financial matters.'

Clare looks shocked.

'What?'

'Quite. I don't know why, nor why Dad didn't tell me about it, but Corrigan showed me his copy and it looked genuine.

'Judging by the date, it must have been set up shortly before the accident.'

'Perhaps Sam didn't mention it because you were in Australia and he thought it would keep until you got back. After all, he wouldn't know he was going to . . .'

'Yes, but that's not all, Clare. Max Corrigan told me Dad got into some sort of investment deal and ended up owing a lot of money. Apparently Corrigan bailed him out. Gave him a loan to pay off the debt.'

'Gosh! That's awful.'

'It's disastrous. And if it's true, it means Corrigan has a stake in the Folly and he clearly means to take full advantage of it.

'He's talking about us working together

to get the business back running. Says he has to look after his investment.'

'It's difficult to believe Sam would have done anything like that.'

'I know. But what on earth does Corrigan want with the Folly?'

'Perhaps there's something we don't know about. Like oil under the rose garden, or buried treasure in the cellar!'

'If only. It doesn't make any sense. I'm praying it's all a mistake.

'Do you think he's trying to con me? I mean, I don't know anything about him and so far I only have his word.'

'There must be some way you can check up on him.'

'I need to talk to Simon. He's been Dad's solicitor for years and I can't imagine him letting Dad do anything silly.'

Clare shakes her head.

'Nor can I. I'm sure once you've seen him and the accountants everything will be clear. If it's genuine, they'll know about it.'

'You're right. I'll get on to it first thing

in the morning.'

'Hey, let's Google this Corrigan chap and see what we can find out about him.'

Why not? It could be interesting.

We take our drinks into the office and Clare fires up the computer. I pull up another chair and sit beside her.

'Do you think his name is Maxwell or just Max?'

'Let's try 'Max Corrigan' and see what that turns up.'

She types it in and a whole page of Corrigans appears. Who would have thought there could be so many Max Corrigans in the world?

'Look at that!' Clare exclaims, pointing to an image of an extremely posh-looking London establishment. 'That can't be him, can it?'

'I reckon he's rich enough.' I think of the suit and the Mercedes.

Then I shake my head.

'But if he was that rich, why would he bother with a run-down country house? Scroll down a bit.'

'How about this? 'Corrigan Financial

Services'?' She clicks on it. 'Actually, he could be any of these. We need a photo.'

'What about that one?' I point to *Corrigan Limousines*.

Clare clicks on the site's images.

'Nope. Not him.'

We scroll down the page looking for details of directors, hoping for photos.

About six down, we find him. Maxwell Corrigan, owner and managing director of Corrigan Enterprises.

One of those enterprises is a chain of luxury hotels spread across the south of England.

'Wow!' Clare says, ogling his image.

'Double wow.' But I'm referring to the business rather than the man.

'Do you think that's him?'

'Oh, it's him all right.'

Clare rolls her eyes.

'I definitely think I should be around when he comes to see you. In case you need a witness or anything, I mean.'

'Clare!' I scowl. 'This man is about to wreck our business and all you can think about is how sexy he is!'

'You don't know he'll do that. He could be perfectly legit and above board. And, if he really has got money invested in the Folly, the last thing he's going to do is jeopardise its success.

'But I would like to know why Sam didn't say anything about him to you.'

'Exactly. Mr Maxwell Corrigan has some explaining to do. But first, I'm going to make that appointment to see Simon tomorrow.'

A Challenge

The following day, Isobel announces her intention to move into the Lodge. I've decided not to say anything to her about Max Corrigan until I know more. There's no point in worrying her needlessly.

'I can't stay in the Folly with all this mess round me,' she declares. 'I don't know what Sam thought he was up to, letting the place go to rack and ruin.'

'Hardly that,' I protest, though she does have a point.

In a way, I'm glad of her decision. Much as I love her, she can be a difficult person to live with and I'm sure we'll both be happier if we are not living on top of each other.

The Lodge isn't nearly as grand as the name implies. It's little more than a two-up, two-down cottage behind the stable yard where some of the outside staff lived when there actually were horses in the stables, in my great-grandparents' time.

Molly has cleaned it and put fresh linen on the bed, so I help Isobel move her belongings across and leave her to settle in.

I need to make a proper inspection of the house, to see what needs doing.

Luckily, I have savings from my Australian job which will tide me over for a while. But it won't last for ever and I need an income.

Though it's lovely to be back in the family home it feels empty without Dad.

I keep expecting to see him around and if I hear a sound somewhere in the house I instinctively think it's him.

I wander around, making lists of everything that needs doing. On the whole, it isn't as bad as I originally thought.

Thanks to Molly, the main hall and dining-room are clean and in good condition, but the bedrooms need some work.

Two could do with a complete overhaul and some will get away with a coat of paint until I can afford to spend more on them.

With a good spring clean, the rest are perfectly useable.

I phone Molly to ask if she can come tomorrow and help me clean and she agrees to come in after lunch. Which reminds me how hungry I am.

I pile some of yesterday's left-overs on a plate, take it through to the hall and curl up on a window-seat to eat.

I've made good progress and, if I can get just half the rooms fit for visitors, I can make enough to keep going for a while.

As soon as probate is through I'll have access to Dad's bank account, plus there will be insurance money which should enable me to do everything necessary to bring the Folly up to standard again.

Clare is coming in tomorrow to sort Dad's papers in the office and get them ready for the solicitor, which will leave Molly and me free to try to restore order to the house.

Things aren't as bad as I'd thought and I'm more optimistic about the future. In fact, I'm looking forward to the challenge.

* * *

I go to my bedroom that night with my mind buzzing with questions.

When we first converted the house to a B&B we moved our bedrooms to the attic floor to leave the best rooms for guests.

The attics are decent-sized rooms, even though the ceilings are a bit low, and I love it up here. They have character and are much cosier than the large rooms below.

I pause outside Dad's room, then go in. It's still painful to be in the room where he slept.

I know I'll have to sort his things soon but I'm not ready yet to go through his clothes and personal items.

It's as he left it and just as I remember, except more untidy than it used to be.

His old towelling dressing-gown lies across the bed. His slippers are on the floor tucked under the chair.

A book is open on the bedside table, next to a glass of water and a pair of spectacles. I didn't even know he wore glasses.

His favourite photos of Mum and me still stand on the shelf opposite. It's as though he is still here.

His desk, where he kept personal papers, stands against the wall next to the window. I run my hand over the smooth polished surface.

I'll have to look inside eventually but right now it seems an intrusion, like breaking into his most private thoughts.

Also, part of me is afraid of what I might find. If Max Corrigan is telling the truth, Dad was in some kind of trouble and, cowardly though it might be, I can't deal with any more shocks.

I'm still reeling from losing him and the odd circumstances of the accident. Because, whatever anyone says, I know he would not have driven off the road like he did without very good reason.

I notice a photograph lying face down on the pillow, as though he had taken it to bed with him. It's of him and Mum just after they were married.

I pick it up and hold it to my chest as if it will bring them nearer.

Oh, Dad, I think. If only you could speak and tell me what happened.

I shiver and realise I'm freezing. I put the photo where I found it and leave the room, shutting the door quietly behind me. I go into my own room next door with questions racing through my mind.

I try to sleep but all I can think about is how Dad got mixed up in money-making schemes. We weren't short of money when I left. Business was good.

Could it have been worry about money that caused the accident? Perhaps he was ill. But there was nothing wrong when I left for Australia or I would never have gone.

And why choose Max Corrigan? Who is this man? Why didn't Dad call me if he had problems? I would have come home.

So many questions. There's definitely something wrong here. I'm certain of it.

Questions follow each other in quick succession as I toss and turn, troubled and unable to sleep.

★ ★ ★

Bleary-eyed from a bad night, I present myself at Simon Shaw's office next morning. He welcomes me with a smile.

'Jessica. Good to see you. How are you?'

'Tired. Relieved to have the funeral over.'

He waves me to a seat.

'It's never an easy time, and flying back at a moment's notice can't have helped.'

I nod.

'I'm only just getting over the jet lag and I still can't get to sleep at a decent hour. I think my body clock is still in Queensland.'

Simon leans back in his chair.

'What can I do for you? Your call made it sound urgent.'

'I want to get the Folly open again for visitors but first I need to know my

41

position regarding finance.'

'We're still waiting on probate but we know Sam left everything to you. Not that there appears to be much, I'm afraid.

'I've had an initial report from the bank and I'm waiting for the rest of the information on his accounts, but I should warn you there may not be a great deal in there.

'It seems Sam withdrew rather a lot from his personal account just before he died.'

That tallies with what Max Corrigan said.

'What about the business account?'

'That's a little healthier but, as I say, we'll know more when the full reports arrive.'

I'm not sure how to put the next question.

'Simon, was there anything wrong with Dad?'

'How do you mean?'

'I had a visit yesterday from a Max Corrigan who gave me a wild story about Dad being in some kind of financial trouble and accepting a loan from him.

42

'What you've just said about him taking money out of his account might have something to do with that.'

'The Max Corrigan who owns the hotel chain?'

'The very same.'

'Well, it's news to me.' Simon shrugs.

'He also said Dad gave him power of attorney to deal with financial matters for him. Why would he do that?'

'It's not unusual. Lots of people make them; it's a sensible thing to do. But Sam said nothing to me about it.

'He could have done it online, though. It's easy and perfectly acceptable.'

'What about the loan? Shouldn't there be an agreement somewhere?'

'I'd say so. I haven't found anything yet, though it may turn up among his papers.'

He indicates a cardboard box on the top of a filing cabinet.

'I have another half dozen of those,' he says, 'full of Sam's papers from the Folly. So far I've only managed to make sense of about a quarter, so there could well be something about a loan among them.

'However, if he did arrange one, he didn't do it through me.'

'Who else would he have gone to?'

'He could have used any solicitor, or it could have been a personal arrangement, in which case I'd have nothing to do with it.'

'Why would he need to give that power to anyone? It's not as if he was ill or old. He was fifty-two, Simon!' I cry. 'And why not give it to me? I just don't understand.'

'Your guess is as good as mine, Jessica. Maybe he felt you were too young.'

'I'm twenty-three. Hardly a child.'

'We'll probably never know now. However, I have heard of Max Corrigan and, from what I hear he's well thought of in the business world.

'Depending on the terms of the loan, there may be implications.'

'That's what worries me. I just wish I knew why Dad did it.'

'Maybe Corrigan will be able to shed

light on the matter. Or perhaps we'll find the answer in one of the boxes.'

'I hope so. Clare is sorting through the office and I'll search the house to see if there's anything there.'

'Let me know if you find anything.'

'I will. Thanks, Simon. Now I'd better get back. I still have a business to rescue and, if I don't start soon, I'll run out of money as well.'

Lunch With the Enemy

I walk to the Lodge to find Isobel. We haven't talked much since the funeral and I want to ask her about Dad.

She left the Folly after Grandpa died and since then she's appeared for occasional holidays, but the rest of the time she spends in her new home on Devon's south coast.

'Much warmer,' she declares, 'and not nearly so wet. It's a great pity Jonas didn't build his house down there.'

She's pottering in the Lodge's tiny cottage garden, pulling out weeds that have sprouted everywhere.

'Hi, Isobel. Do you have everything you need?'

She straightens up, rubbing her back.

'I'm fine, thank you, Jessica. Which is more than I can say for this place.'

She waves her arm towards the cottage.

'When did your father last do any maintenance work round here?'

'Good question. I'm not sure what he did or didn't do while I was away.'

She looks hard at me.

'What's up? You look as if the world's about to end.'

'Actually, it feels rather like it.'

Yesterday's revelations, together with the visit to Simon, are beginning to take their toll on me.

I swipe my hand across my eyes as she puts her arms round me.

'Whatever is it, dear? I suppose you're feeling Sam's loss. They say it takes time to really hit you.

'I don't suppose you've had time to properly grieve, with everything you've had to deal with. I haven't been much help, have I?'

She gives me a big hug and releases me.

'Come inside and I'll put the kettle on. We'll have a nice cup of tea.'

I smile at her.

'That would be lovely.'

Isobel can be quite human sometimes. I've always suspected she hides a soft centre under that fierce exterior she shows to the world.

She has lit a fire and the sitting-room is warm and cosy and very welcoming. I settle on the ancient sofa and curl my legs under me.

Watching the flames reminds me of childhood and sitting with Mum in front of the fire in the hall, watching fairies flickering on the fire back.

What wouldn't I give to have Mum back?

Isobel comes in with the tea tray and puts it on the table in front of the sofa.

'Do you realise, Jessica, you and I are the last of our family?' she says as if she can read my mind. 'It's just you and me now.'

'I was thinking the same. It's hard to believe, isn't it, when there were once so many of us?'

'Far too many, I used to think sometimes!'

'I remember when Great-gran was still alive. There was her, Grandpa and Grandma, you and Uncle Rob, and Dad and Mum. Four generations, all living here together.

'It's a pity Dad was an only child or I might have had cousins. That would have been nice.'

Isobel tuts.

'It's a miracle even your father managed to make an appearance. Your grandmother was too busy entertaining and enjoying the high life to have time for children. It was a great disappointment to us all.'

'And Mum being ill meant I was an only child, too,' I murmur.

'So here we are, just the two of us.'

Isobel picks up the tea pot and pours. She seems surprisingly emotional. Perhaps family means more to her than she lets on.

'Now,' she says, handing me a cup and settling herself in the easy chair next to the fire. 'What has upset you?'

I tell her what I know. As I go through it all again, it seems even more out of character for Dad.

'That is outrageous!' Isobel declares.

'Whatever was the man thinking of? Always assuming this Corrigan person is telling the truth, of course.'

'It's hard to believe, isn't it?'

'You say the solicitor knows nothing about it?'

'Well, he hasn't found anything yet but there are lots more papers to go through. He has boxes of them.

'I haven't been through Dad's room yet. I can't bring myself to look into his personal things. It feels so intrusive.'

'Well, you'll have to tackle it sometime. Who knows what he might have hidden away? Would you like me to help you?'

I shake my head.

'Do you mind if I say no? I feel it's something I need to do on my own.'

'I understand. But don't leave it too long. There could be important documents there that can throw some light on this puzzle.'

'You're right. I promise I'll do it soon.'

★ ★ ★

The answering machine is blinking as I go into the kitchen. I hit the *play* button and hear Max Corrigan telling me he'll be dropping in to see me this afternoon.

I suppose this is the follow-up call he promised after our meeting. Surely he could have given me more notice!

But that's probably typical of the man. He clearly thinks the hold he has over my home and my bank account gives him the right to appear whenever it suits him, whether it fits with my plans or not.

I suppose that's what running a high-powered enterprise does to you.

He hasn't even given a time. How arrogant! I expect he sees the Folly as a potential take-over to add to his multi-million chain, with me on hand to do his bidding.

Well, he has another think coming. I intend to make absolutely sure he realises this is my business, not his!

I glance at the clock and wonder if I have time to grab a quick bite of lunch before he turns up. I set the coffee-machine going and find some cheese and pickle in the fridge to make a sandwich.

I've just taken a large bite when the doorbell rings. Darn it, it's not even one o'clock. Doesn't the man eat lunch?

Cursing him, I hastily swallow, put a plate over the rest of the sandwich and stick it back in the fridge.

I open the door just as he's lifting his hand to ring again.

'Ah, you are in, then,' he says. 'I wasn't sure if you'd have got my message.'

'About five minutes ago. I do have a life apart from you, you know.'

'I apologise. I just happen to have a free afternoon.'

He doesn't look very sorry.

'What can I do for you?'

'Aren't you going to ask me in?'

'Must I?'

I know I'm being rude but I really don't want this meeting and having my lunch interrupted has not improved my mood.

'No,' he says, 'but it will be easier to discuss matters inside than standing on the doorstep.'

Grudgingly I step back and let him into the hall. I close the door and wait.

If he thinks I'm going to invite him any further, he's mistaken.

'So, what do we have to discuss?' I ask. He sighs.

'Look, I know this has been a shock for you but, believe me, the problems are not of my making. It will make life easier for us both if we can at least be polite to each other.'

'Well, it's certainly none of my doing!' I snap back. 'So who exactly is responsible for this ridiculous situation?'

'I think you might find it's your father.'

Suddenly I'm afraid he might be telling me the truth and I lose the urge to fight him.

Can I trust this man? Dad appears to have done so and Simon said he has a good reputation. Perhaps he's on the level.

'Look,' he continues, 'I don't know about you but I could use a coffee. What do you say we go and make one? Then we can snap each other's heads off in comfort.'

To my annoyance, I can't help smiling. He's right, I'm achieving nothing by keeping him standing in the hall and throwing a verbal tantrum.

This has to be sorted and I suppose we might as well co-operate as fight each other.

But that doesn't mean I'm letting my guard down. I intend to watch Max Corrigan very carefully indeed.

We go to the kitchen where he leans against the Aga, looking irritatingly comfortable and at home, while I add another cup to the coffee-machine.

'If the rest of the house is anything like this room,' he says, 'it must be pretty special.'

'It is.' The fact that he appreciates the house is a tiny notch in his favour.

'It looks old,' he says, looking up at the beamed ceiling.

'Not really. It's early Victorian; built by my several-times-great-grandfather in 1840, so not as old as it looks.'

'If it's been in your family all that time,

I can see why it means so much to you.'

Another small crack opens in my defences. Under different circumstances I could like this man.

My stomach rumbles and I remember my sandwich.

'Do you mind if I finish my lunch?' I ask, retrieving it from the fridge.

'Feel free.'

Now I'm embarrassed. I can't very well stand here eating in front of him so I offer to make him one.

'Thank you. I'd like that.'

'Perhaps you could pour the coffee while I do it?'

This is crazy. A few moments ago I didn't want him in the house. Now I'm making him lunch.

While we eat I sneak a look at him and wonder what it takes to build a business the size of his. Or maybe he inherited it? I'll have to do some more Googling.

The photo on his website doesn't do him justice. He really is very attractive. That thick, dark hair, just a tad too long, that lean face with that intriguing little scar.

Not handsome, exactly, but . . .

Suddenly he looks straight at me and I flush. Was he aware of me looking at him? Oh, I hope not.

He smiles and I'm sure my flush deepens. Angry for having let him get to me, I gather our plates and mugs and take them to the sink, hoping my face's colour will return to normal.

'Why don't you tell me why you're here?' I suggest, keeping my back to him. 'I assume you didn't just come to have lunch with me?'

'Enjoyable though it has been, I'm afraid not. I'm here because, whether you like it or not, between us we have a business to run and the sooner we get started the better.'

'Hold on a minute.' I turn and face him. 'Let's get something straight right now. I have a business to run.

'The business and this house are mine, not yours. I would appreciate it if you could remember that.'

His eyes darken with anger and I know a momentary flash of fear. I should be more careful. He could be a violent man. I have no way of knowing.

His voice is dangerously low as he responds.

'To be perfectly accurate, Miss Flynn, you have a majority share of a business to run. I also have a substantial share in it as one of your major creditors and, until the loan I made to your father is repaid, I intend to make sure my investment does not go the way the rest of your father's money went.

'So it really would be to your advantage for us to remain civil and find some way of working together.'

He's right, of course. I may not like it but there's nothing to be gained by closing my eyes to the facts.

'Right,' I say through gritted teeth. 'Thank you for putting it so succinctly. I can see you have me over the proverbial barrel so how about telling me exactly how much you do have invested in the Folly?'

He takes a document from the inside pocket of his jacket.

'I've brought you a copy of our agreement, in case you haven't yet found Sam's.'

I take it and my heart sinks when I see the amount of money involved.

'Good grief! So much?'

'I'm afraid so.'

I fold the paper and put it down on the table.

'However am I going to repay that sort of money?'

'We'll find a way. If I wasn't sure of getting my money back I wouldn't have invested it. You have a lot of potential here but it needs managing and developing properly.'

I think I've lost the will to fight him.

'OK, I'm listening, but I need to know more.'

He relaxes into his chair and the atmosphere clears a little.

'Believe it or not, I don't know much more about how he got into this mess than you do.

'Your father and mine knew each other from way back when they were members

58

of the same branch of the Federation of Small Businesses. They kept in touch but my father hadn't heard from Sam for several years, until he called him a couple of months ago and asked if he could come and see him.'

'I never heard Dad mention anyone called Corrigan.'

'He might have done if you'd been here at the time.'

I feel a twinge of guilt and react angrily.

'Dad was perfectly happy for me to go to Australia! In fact, he encouraged me to go.'

'Calm down. I'm not accusing you of anything. I'm just saying, had you been here, Sam would no doubt have told you what he was doing.'

'Why didn't he write or phone me, though? Even the outback has modern communications.'

Dad could have got in touch easily. It's as if he didn't want me to know what he was doing, and that wasn't like him. We always shared everything.

'We may never know the reason,' Max

replies.

'Doesn't your father have any ideas?'

'Neither of us has. All we know is something was worrying Sam enough for him to want some kind of help. I don't know why he didn't want to go into detail as to the reason.'

'And you were prepared to lend him a large amount of money without knowing why?'

'In return for a share of the business. He gave the house as collateral. It was all properly set up.

'I had my solicitor draw up an agreement which we both signed but, at Sam's request, I kept it as a personal arrangement between us.'

Another thought occurs to me.

'Who arranged the power of attorney? It wasn't Dad's solicitor so I suppose it was yours?'

'No, Sam was adamant he wanted to keep it quiet so he did it all online. Because my father knew him well, I didn't see a problem.'

'Why you? Why not your father, if they

are friends?'

'It was agreed I would be better able to help as I'm involved in the same line of business.'

I laugh bitterly.

'Hardly. We looked you up on Google. I would say your line of business is a million miles away from the Folly.'

He shrugs.

'Not so distant. The principle is the same. Now, can we accept we need to work together on this?'

Grudgingly, I agree.

'I suppose I have no choice.'

'Not much, I'm afraid.'

'So where do we start?'

'Why don't we begin with a guided tour? I love the look of this house and it will help me get a better idea of the situation.'

A Brilliant Idea

We stop to look at the portrait of Jonas hanging at the foot of the main stairs.

'Jonas Flynn,' I tell him. 'The man who built this house.'

Max Corrigan looks from the portrait to me and back again.

'I can't see a family likeness.'

'I take after my mother. We got the short, fair genes.'

He looks as if he's about to say something but changes his mind.

'Tell me about Jonas.'

'I can't tell you much. How he came here and even how he built the house is a bit of a mystery.

'We know the stone was quarried from the hill behind the house. Family legend has it that other materials and labour were paid for with proceeds from smuggling, which was rife in those days.

'Whether Jonas took an active part in smuggling or just turned a blind eye, as many people did, we don't know, but he clearly did well for himself.

'He managed to acquire six acres of land and, against all odds, it's been in the family ever since.'

'Quite a character.'

We go into the main hall where we'd gathered after the funeral. It's looking beautiful, sun shining through the tall windows, and I can tell this man is impressed.

My grandparents hosted the hunt ball here one year. I'd sat at the top of the stairs looking down at the glamorous women and their partners and wishing I could join them.

By the time I was old enough to do so, the family finances had declined to the point where, in an effort to save our home, my parents were considering opening it to paying guests.

We move through to the small sitting-room, Grandpa's retreat when life became too hectic. My grandmother was never happier than when surrounded by friends and neighbours but Grandpa and his brother, Rob, who lived with us, preferred dogs and horses to people; something Dad and I inherited from them.

We finish downstairs and go up the front staircase to the first floor.

'How many bedrooms are there?'

'Eight on this floor. There are four attic ones but two we only use for storage. The roof leaks a bit when we get a storm.'

We go into the room that had been my parents' until Dad moved to the attic.

'This is our best letting-room.'

It will always be Mum and Dad's room to me and it holds many precious memories.

Like when, as a child, I'd come in on Christmas mornings to sit on the bed and open the presents in my stocking.

Or sometimes in the middle of the night, after a bad dream, I'd run in and was allowed to cuddle up between them.

Then the times when I sat here with Mum during the last days of her life . . .

'Four bedrooms are en-suite,' I explain.

'Not good. They should all be.'

I glare at him.

'Just don't forget whose house this is.'

'You need me, remember, if you are going to keep it.'

I grit my teeth.

'Look, I know this is difficult for you but it'll be easier for us both if we co-operate. For the time being, at least, it really is in your interest to let me help.'

I want to strangle him. Somehow, I must find a way out of this mess on my own.

But there's the spectre of that loan hanging over me. How can I repay that except by making a success of the business?

And for that I need his help.

We return to the hall.

'Have you seen enough?' I ask him. 'Or would you like a tour of the cellars?'

He chuckles.

'I'll pass on that, thank you, but I'd like to see the gardens. It would help me get a picture of what we have to work with and there might be potential for extra income.'

'Such as a swimming-pool or golf course?'

He doesn't rise to the bait.

'A golf course might be a little ambitious, don't you think?' he replies calmly.

We take the path round the house to the terrace where Dad and I had often sat in the evenings looking out over the sea, and where guests walked after dinner or enjoyed afternoon tea.

Max halts and looks round.

'This is some view! You know, you have a potential goldmine here. Think about it. It's a secluded position in glorious countryside.

'You have the moor for a back garden, the sea within walking distance and, if you just want to laze, you can sit here and soak up the scenery. Why on earth aren't you making a small fortune out of this place?'

He has a point. We should be. In fact, we were well on the way to doing just that.

We had solid bookings, good reviews

on all the websites and money in the bank.

Again, I ask myself what went wrong.

'I don't know. I wish I did.'

'Cheer up. I'm beginning to have a good feeling about this. Take me on a tour of the estate and let's see what we've got.'

We leave the terrace and walk down the drive towards the stable yard. As we pass the track to the Lodge, Max pauses.

'What's that? Does it belong to you?'

'It's where the yard workers lived when we had horses. Apart from the occasional short-term let, we don't use it much.'

'Have you considered making it into a holiday cottage?'

'It would need improvement first.'

'Can we look round?'

'My aunt is staying there at the moment so I'd rather not.'

'Another day, perhaps.'

We move on into the yard.

'I take it there are no horses at the moment.'

'What do you think? Horses cost

money, lots of it. The last time this place saw a horse was when my uncle kept his hunters here years ago.

'The only equines here now are two Exmoor ponies and they live out all year so cost next to nothing. In fact, they earn their keep by keeping the grass in check.'

'Where are they now?'

'I left them with a friend while I was away. I haven't had a chance to collect them yet.'

It would be wonderful to have horses in the yard again. I have such happy memories of when Uncle Rob lived in the house and his horses were here in the stables. The yard was a hive of activity.

We move on, past the old kennels.

'My great-great-grandfather kept a pack of hounds. These haven't been used as kennels for years and are just a general dumping place for stuff from the house.'

'There must be something more constructive you could do with this area than just using it as storage.'

'Maybe.' I wonder how much this city

man can know about life in the country.

I take him past the field where the ponies will be when I bring them back. It's wet and muddy from recent rain and the stream that flows along one side has overflowed its banks again, adding to the mud.

I really must get it cleared out.

We finish our tour and Max leaves, promising to be in touch again soon.

And then I realise that for the last hour I've been thinking of him as Max.

★ ★ ★

I go back to the house, thinking. Walking round the yard has given me an idea that grows until, by the time I reach the office, I'm certain I've found the perfect solution.

Clare, busy on the computer, looks up.

'For someone who's just spent the best part of the afternoon with the most hated man in her life, you look remarkably cheery.

'I think I have the answer to our problems!'

'You've dug up that long-lost treasure the pirates buried under the mulberry tree?'

'Better than that.'

'You've won the lottery?'

'I wish. Sadly, no.'

'OK, I give in. Tell me.'

'Remember this?'

I point to a photo hanging on the wall; one taken by Dad the day Uncle Rob gave me my first riding lesson.

I'm five years old, sitting on Monty, my first Exmoor pony.

'Vaguely,' Clare says. 'If you remember, I wasn't keen on riding. Anyway, what has an old photo to do with your rescue plan?

'Do you remember what it was like when Uncle Rob had his horses here? The place was always buzzing with people and sometimes he had friends to stay overnight with their horses.'

Those were some of the happiest days of my life. Uncle had employed a boy from the village to look after the yard and, as soon as I was old enough, I'd spent all my free time there helping with the horses.

'I'm not following you, Jess. You can't afford to buy horses, nor keep them.'

'I know that.'

'Well, don't keep me in suspense!'

'We are going to do riding holidays. Isn't that a great idea?'

Clare looks at me as if I'm mad.

'We are going to do what?'

I say it again.

'That's what I thought you said. Where are we going to get horses from? Or riding instructors? And what about the state of the stables? They are virtually falling down.

I refuse to let her dampen my enthusiasm.

'I know all that, but we won't need to provide any of it — apart from the stables, of course. Guests will look after their own mounts. We run it like a DIY livery.

'Think about it. Here we are in the middle of glorious riding country. We have the moor, woods and coast, criss-crossed with miles of bridleways.

'No main roads to cope with. They can go straight from here on to some of the best riding country in England. What more could any rider want? And if they need a guide, I'll take them out.'

I can see from Clare's expression I'm beginning to get through to her.

'What do you think? It'll bring the place to life again. Just like the old days. Lots of people enjoy riding holidays with their own horse.'

'I still think you're mad.' She begins to smile. 'But you might just have something worth looking into.'

I stand up and punch the air.

'Yes! We can do this, I know we can. Is it too early for a celebration drink?'

Clare frowns.

'It most certainly is. It's no more than an idea right now. Those stables need a lot of work and, whether you want to admit it or not, it'll take shed-loads of money.'

'I shall go and see Giles.'

Why didn't I think of that before? Giles owns the extremely upmarket

Mermaid at the harbour. He's a bit of a wheeler-dealer but he knows how to make money and he's rolling in it.

He'll know what I need to do. And I won't have to go to Max Corrigan.

Clare's not looking happy.

'All right,' I say. 'What's wrong with that?'

'I don't like Giles. More to the point, I don't trust him.'

'Whyever not?'

'I don't know. He was round here a lot while you were away. Sam said he was helping him, but . . .'

'But what? There's no reason Giles shouldn't have been here. Perhaps Dad wanted advice.'

Clare shrugs.

'The thing is, Sam never seemed happy after Giles had been. In fact, there were times when he looked really worried.

'I may be wrong but, now I think about it, I'm wondering if Giles could have been the cause of Sam's worry rather than helping him.'

It isn't like my friend to imagine

things, or take a dislike to anyone without cause. Clare's one of those people who gets on with everyone, so, if she thinks she sensed something wrong, I'm inclined to believe her instincts.

But it can't have been Giles. It must have been something else; something Giles was helping Dad with.

'All the more reason for me to go and see him.'

Untrustworthy

I walk to Larkcombe harbour to see Giles. It's a crisp, bright autumn morning and with a renewed sense of optimism I stride down the combe to Larkcombe village and along the bridleway that snakes through oak and birch woods down to the harbour.

The sun flashes and sparkles through the branches and birds sing overhead. For the first time since coming home, I'm feeling relaxed.

The Mermaid stands across the road from the harbour wall, facing the sea. It's mostly 17th century with Georgian additions and by far the most impressive building here.

The hotel is as smart and expensive as its clientèle and the Folly, in contrast, seems shabby and run down.

I feel guilty at this thought, but it makes me realise how much Dad has let it go while I've been away.

I cross the road and go through the

main entrance to reception. Sally is still here at the desk and she comes over and gives me a hug.

'Jess, it's lovely to see you. Love the tan! How was Australia?'

'Wonderful. But it's good to be back.'

'I was so sorry to hear about your dad. How are things at the Folly?'

I grimace.

'Long story, I'm afraid; which is why I'm here. Is Giles in?'

'In his office. I'll give him a buzz.'

I look at the expensively decorated and furnished hall. If only I could make the Folly as good as this. It might cater for a completely different clientèle but there's no reason why it shouldn't have the same high standards.

Sally comes back.

'Go through. He's expecting you.'

I walk along the plushly carpeted corridor to Giles's office and knock on the open door. He looks up from his desk and stands to meet me.

'Jessica! How lovely to see you. Come in.'

He kisses my cheek.

'You look well.'

'It's good to see you, too, Giles.'

'I'm sorry I haven't been over to see you.' He pulls out a chair for me to sit down. 'I've been tied up with things here.'

'No problem, I understand. I hope you don't mind me calling?'

'Of course not. How are you? You must be relieved to have the funeral over, but it was good to see so many people there.'

'Yes. It was.'

'What a shock it was for everyone,' Giles continues. 'And for you as well, of course. So completely unexpected.

'If there's anything I can do to help, you must let me know. There must be all sorts of business matters to sort out.'

'Thank you. Actually, there is something you can help me with, Giles.'

'Anything. With all the estate matters you'll have a lot to cope with and I'll be only too happy to take some of it off your shoulders.

'You are Sam's executor, I take it?'

'No, thank goodness. Simon is dealing with all that.'

A look of unease flashes across Giles's face but it's gone in an instant and I decide I must have imagined it.

He smiles.

'Forgive me, I'm forgetting my manners. Let me send for some refreshment. What would you like?'

'Something cold, please. I walked from the Folly.'

I wait while he buzzes for drinks. Sally brings a tray of real lemonade and Giles pours for us both.

'Here's to you, Jessica,' he says, clinking his glass against mine. 'Now, tell me what I can do for you.'

'I need advice on a project I have in mind. Clare says you'd been talking to Dad so you must have a pretty good idea of the situation. You'll be aware I need to do something pretty quick if I'm to revive the business.'

He drains his glass and gives me his full attention.

'You're right. I did go up to see Sam

once or twice, at his request, and I suspected all was not well.'

'I agree. I think something was very wrong, but I've no idea what. I thought it might help if you can tell me why he wanted to see you?'

I catch again that fleeting expression of unease. He covers it by pouring another drink before answering but it's clear he's also worried about something.

'I honestly don't know, Jessica,' he says finally. 'He just seemed to want to talk but it was never about anything specific.'

'So you have no idea?'

'None at all, I'm afraid.'

I've been pinning my hopes on Giles throwing some light on the matter but it looks as if he knows no more than I do.

In which case, why do I have the feeling he's uncomfortable about something?

I'm sure there's more to this than he's letting on, but I can see I'm not going to get anything further out of him at the moment. I shall have to bide my time.

'That's a shame,' I say, 'but if you do think of anything, perhaps you could let me know.'

I decide to change the subject.

'That wasn't the only reason for coming to see you,' I tell him. 'I'd like to talk to you about a plan I have for the Folly.'

He looks more comfortable now.

'By all means. Go ahead.'

'As I say, I have to do something to revitalise the business and attract visitors, but I need more than just bed-and-breakfast guests.

'There's hardly any money in the bank. I've no idea why, but the fact remains I appear to be nearly broke. I can't run the Folly on thin air so I have to do something that will really bring in the money.'

Giles frowns.

'I'd no idea it was that bad. I wish Sam had told me he was in trouble. I'd have been only too pleased to help.'

'It's a mystery to me, too.'

'So?'

'I have a plan I think can save us but I need an unbiased opinion from someone who understands both the implications and the business. As you've known Dad for ages I thought I might run it past you.'

He lounges back in his chair and folds his arms.

'I'm intrigued. Fire away.'

I explain what I have in mind and wait for him to say something, but he's not looking responsive.

'You don't like it?' I ask eventually when he still hasn't spoken.

He frowns.

'I just wonder if you aren't trying to take on too much. It will take a lot of hard work and money. And will it bring the income you need?'

I was expecting a little more enthusiasm. I feel deflated and answer more abruptly than I intend.

'Well, thanks for the encouragement, Giles. I'm perfectly aware it will be hard work but I'm not afraid of that. And I know it can work if I can just get it up and running.

'I'd hoped for something a little more positive from you, I must say.'

'I applaud your enthusiasm, Jessica,

but I don't think you've thought this through. Supposing it could bring you the return you need, how will you fund it? You say you have no money in the bank.'

'There is some, just not very much. I'm hoping it will be enough for a deposit so I can get a loan.

'Then there's Dad's insurance, when it comes through. That should pay for some of the work.

'I was hoping you could advise me on how to go about it, but you clearly think it's a lost cause before I've even started!'

I realise I'm raising my voice and make an effort to stay calm.

'Of course,' he says, 'I'll do what I can, but I'm not happy about you taking on a project like that.'

'Why not? I have to do something and what else is there? I have to make a living somehow from the Folly if I'm going to be able to keep it.

'It's my home, Giles. I have to find a way.'

There's a lump in my throat and I

pray I'm not going to cry. Giles is looking uncomfortable as if he's afraid I'm going to make a scene.

'OK, OK,' he says. 'Fine. I can see you're determined so let me think about it.'

It's not the reaction I'd hoped for but at least he's agreeing to think it over. There has to be a way forward without relying on Max.

Which, I remember, is something else I want to ask Giles.

'Giles, did Dad say anything to you about a power of attorney?'

'Not that I recall. Why?'

I tell him and his expression darkens.

'What is it?' I ask. 'What do you know?'

He frowns.

'I have no idea why Sam did it, but I have heard of Max Corrigan and I'm sorry to say I certainly wouldn't trust him.

'You should be very careful if you have dealings with him, Jessica. You know how he built that empire of his? By buying out the competition at rock-bottom prices when they were in trouble.'

I'm surprised at the vehemence in Giles' voice. Whatever else I might think about Max, I'd come to the conclusion he was honest and I find myself defending him.

'Surely there is nothing wrong with that? It's what happens in business. If they were struggling, they were probably glad to have someone buy them out.

'Better than having to declare bankruptcy, anyway. '

'Maybe, but there are ways and there are ways. Some are more honourable than others.'

I find it difficult to believe Max would be part of anything shady but I determine to look into it further when I get home. Maybe I'll ask Simon to check him out more thoroughly.

Right now I think it's time I left. I'm not sure why, but I'm not feeling comfortable discussing Max like this.

I stand up.

'Thanks for listening, Giles. I'll think about what you've said.'

He walks me to the door and holds it open for me.

'I'm sorry if I sounded a bit off about your idea, Jessica. I feel I owe it to Sam to keep a watchful eye. I promise I'll give your plan some serious thought and I'll be in touch.'

I leave, disappointed with Giles's response. I'd expected him to be more supportive.

I replay our conversation in my mind and can't help feeling he over-reacted, but I can't think of any reason why he should.

So maybe I'm imagining things, but between Max Corrigan and Giles, I'm feeling more confused than ever.

* * *

I'm not far from Emma's place so I decide to collect the ponies and ride Freddy home. Emma and I were at school together, and she and her husband, Bill, farm the fields next to mine.

She also runs a small riding school

and she's been looking after my boys for me. She isn't around when I get there so I text her to let her know I'm taking Freddy.

Both ponies are as pleased to see me as I am to see them and I'm subjected to a boisterous group cuddle.

I saddle Freddy and Monty protests loudly when he realises he's being left behind, but he's far too old for hard exercise and I'm looking forward to a good run over the moor.

I decide to take the long way home, up over the hill behind the harbour and along the ridge so I can come down the combe to the Folly.

It feels good to be back in the saddle. Freddy is sure-footed and knows the paths well so I switch off and let my mind wander. I have plenty to think about, following my talk with Giles.

We climb through ancient oak woods to the top of the steep incline and emerge on to the open moor. At first, Freddy's bouncy pony gait feels strange after the long, loping strides of the big Australian cattle horses I've been riding over the past months.

I enjoyed Australia but for sheer beauty Exmoor beats it hands down. In the bright autumn sun every contour of the vast rolling landscape stands out in relief.

Great rounded clumps of yellow gorse glow against the darkening purple heather.

It's another world up here, a world where it's almost possible to forget the problems of everyday life altogether.

I urge Freddy into a canter. He doesn't need much encouragement and we soon reach the top of Larkcombe combe. I pull him up and sit looking at the village far below.

Beyond the village, fields golden with ripe barley sprawl northwards to meet the marsh where the land surrenders to the sea at every high tide.

Emotion courses through me. This place is where I belong and, come hell or high water, this is where I am going to stay.

Somehow, I'll find a way to save the Folly.

I give Freddy his head and let him pick his way down the steep stony bridleway. Halfway down, we turn through a gate and enter the woods that border our land.

As the house comes into view, I feel a surge of pride and make a silent promise to myself, to Jonas and to all my family that I will not give up.

There is, as Giles has so bluntly pointed out, much to be done.

Missing Money

I ride Freddy into the yard, unsaddle him, brush him down and let him loose in his old paddock. He sniffs the air, then races away across the field, bucking and kicking up his heels.

'Good to be home, isn't it?' I say, smiling at his antics.

He whinnies agreement then drops his head and begins the serious business of feeding.

'We'll fetch your pal tomorrow,' I tell him.

I lean on the gate and watch him for a while, dreaming about the future.

'Hi! Jess!'

Startled back to the present I look up, to see Emma coming down the lane.

'Thought I'd come and say hello,' she says. 'I see you've brought Freddy back. When did you want to fetch Monty?'

'As soon as I can arrange it. He'll be unhappy left on his own.'

'I have to come this way tomorrow. I

can drop him off for you.'

'That would be marvellous, Em.

'I don't suppose you have time for a cuppa, do you? There's something I'd like to talk to you about.'

'Sounds wonderful. I haven't had a chance to see you since the funeral and it's time we had a good natter.'

I should have thought of Emma before. She's the obvious person to talk to. She's had years of experience with horses and with running a business.

Who needs Giles or Max? With Emma's help I can do perfectly well without either of them.

Emma follows me into the kitchen and I fill the coffee-machine and find half a packet of chocolate biscuits. Then I tell her what I'm planning to do.

By the time we've finished our first mug of coffee and most of the biscuits Emma is hooked.

'It's a brilliant idea, Jess!'

'You really think so?'

'Of course! It's the obvious answer. Apart from some work on the stables, you already have everything you need in place.'

I could hug her. Her enthusiasm is so different from Giles's reaction.

'You don't know what a relief it is to hear you say that,' I tell her. 'It won't affect your business, will it?'

It has just occurred to me that it might take trade away from Emma, which is the last thing I want to do.

'I don't see why it should,' she says. 'We'll be offering two completely different things. It might even bring me some new customers.'

'You mean, if some of my guests need riding instruction, who better to go to than you?' I nod.

'Right, and I might be able to send some people to you for accommodation.'

'Great!'

'Fantastic!'

I laugh. I put the lid back on the biscuit tin. Who needs comfort food? Everything is going swimmingly.

'Tell you what,' I say, 'let's go and look at the stables.'

Emma grins.

'Strike while the iron's hot and all that? Lead on, partner.'

We walk down the drive and into the yard. I haven't looked at the buildings — really looked at them properly — for a good couple of years. I didn't realise they are in such poor condition.

Because we haven't had horses here for so long, they have just been forgotten. When Dad and I were running the place on our own, it was a case of doing what had to be done and leaving anything we felt wasn't vital. Like the stables.

Two rows of six boxes face each other across a central cobbled area. Weeds are growing among the cobbles and I feel guilty we've let them get in such a state.

Grandpa and Uncle Rob would be horrified to see them as they are now.

I groan.

'I didn't realise it was such a mess. Where on earth do we start?'

'At the beginning,' Emma replies. 'Cheer up. All it needs is enthusiasm and hard work. It's a great idea! Come on, let's have a look.'

An hour later, as we sit on the steps of the old mounting block, I'm not sure enthusiasm and hard work is going to be enough.

Every door needs replacing, part of the roof needs repairing and the whole place needs a thorough clean. It's going to cost far more than I anticipated.

'Jim might help. I was going to ask him if he'll paint the bedrooms and he's always looking for odd jobs.' I sigh. 'Just one problem, though. I don't have any money.'

'What? None?'

'Only my earnings from Australia and they'll have to cover day-to-day expenses for the foreseeable future.'

'But Sam must have money in the bank?'

'Not much and I can't access it anyway until probate is through.'

'How long will that be?'

'I've no idea. Simon is still collecting everything together. Dad wasn't the tidiest of people and he didn't plan on leaving us when he did.'

There is, of course, one source of funding, but it's one I don't want to use.

'There is Max,' I mutter.

'Who's Max?' I realise Emma has no idea who I'm talking about.

'Goodness,' she says when I've explained. 'How odd. But he's the obvious person to go to. Surely he'll be happy to pay for renovations.'

'I don't want to involve him any more than I have to. I can't explain, but I need to do this without him.'

'I don't see the problem. From what you say, all he's tried to do so far is help you and fulfil an obligation to Sam.

'What do you have against him, Jess?'

'He's overbearing and interfering and wants to take charge. He talks of the Folly as if we're partners.

'It's 'we'll do this' and 'we'll do that'. He just makes me mad!'

Emma laughs.

'It seems to me the lady doth protest too much.'

'Oh, no. Don't read anything into this

that isn't there. I absolutely do not feel anything for him.'

Of course I don't. Heavens, I hardly know the man.

I jump up.

'Enough of Max Corrigan. If I can just hold out until probate is through, I'll have the insurance money. I know Dad was well covered.

'Then I won't need to ask anyone, Max or Giles. I shall go to the bank tomorrow and find out exactly what the situation is.'

'Good idea. And good luck, Jess. Whatever I can do to help, I will.'

'I'm determined to do this, Em. One way or another.'

* * *

The following morning I phone the bank and make an appointment to see the manager towards the end of the afternoon.

Clare is busy sorting through papers in the office.

'I've been going through the books, Jess. A lot of the records are with the accountants and solicitors, but from what I've seen, the situation isn't too bad.

'We were still taking in guests until a couple of weeks before Sam died and the income from that shows in the books together with the usual outgoings.

'However, there is something odd. In his personal cheque book there are several large amounts made out to cash.'

I frown.

'Simon said there were some big payments going out but he didn't know what they were for. Wouldn't you have known about them if you were doing the books, Clare?'

'Not if they were private cheques.'

She shows me the cheque book. It's Dad's writing, all right, but what did he do with such huge sums of money?

It's with some trepidation I enter the manager's office later that day.

He shakes my hand and waves me to a seat.

'My condolences on your loss, Miss Flynn. How can I help you?'

'Thank you. To put it bluntly, Mr Stevens, I need to know how much money I have and how soon I can draw some of it out.'

He consults the computer on the desk in front of him.

'I'm afraid,' he says, 'your father's account is not looking healthy. I did make the situation clear to your solicitor.

'There's a little left in the business account, but he withdrew several large amounts from his personal account in the days before he died.

'There will, of course, be adjustments to be made as his executors finalise his affairs, but I'm afraid it won't make much difference to the end result.'

I'm appalled.

'Are you telling there is nothing in his accounts?'

'Not nothing, but certainly not very much. I estimate you will have one, perhaps two thousand in total.'

I take a deep breath as the shock hits

me. I hadn't expected a fortune, but to be told I have so little is scary.

'But he paid money into the account!' I say. 'We have the paying-in books. His bookkeeper has the records.'

'Yes, he did. But for some reason he also took most of it out again in that final week.'

'Where did it go?'

'He withdrew it as cash so I have no way of knowing.'

'How am I supposed to keep going without money? I need funds to make repairs and pay bills.'

'Surely there'll be insurance money, if nothing else?'

'Very likely, but that will be dealt with by the executors and I have no idea how much it will be.'

This is not looking good, but I still have high hopes for the riding holidays. I brace myself to ask the question.

'Mr Stevens, I do have a plan for attracting more guests and reviving the business.'

'I'm pleased to hear it. I wish you success.'

I'm sure he knows what I'm going to ask.

'The thing is, I'm a little short of funds at the moment — well, you know that, of course. So I was wondering if I can get a small loan to enable me to set it up?'

'Not without some income, I'm afraid. And you'll need a deposit. Or a guarantor.'

'I see.'

'Is there anything else I can do for you?' he asks.

What else can he do for me?

'No, thank you.' I stand up. 'I guess that's it, then.'

'I'm very sorry, Miss Flynn. If there is anything I can do to help, please let me know.'

'How about you magic up some money?'

He smiles sympathetically as he shows me to the door.

Disappointed, I make my way back to my car and drive home.

Under the Influence

I get back to find Clare has already left so, despite the early hour, I pour a large glass of red wine. Taking the bottle with me, I curl up on the sofa and spend the next hour watching some mindless TV programme and feeling sorry for myself.

I hardly register what I'm watching. All I can think of is how I'm going to manage. On top of the shock of losing Dad, it's too much to take in. Too much to deal with.

As the wine slowly works its magic I start to unwind. This isn't like me. I'm not a person who sits feeling sorry for herself.

I give myself a mental shake. OK, so there's no money in the bank; but I have the house and I have a business. One that is, admittedly, pretty moribund, but I can change that. I'll renovate the stables.

I'll bring the Folly back to life.

I'm sober enough to realise this might partly be the wine talking, but what does that matter if it snaps me out of the doldrums?

I need income. I need visitors. I need a plan.

Firstly, deal with the bedrooms; decorate where necessary and start advertising again.

It needn't cost the earth. I can do much of the work myself. After all, I once helped Dad paint the whole house.

I only need enough money to buy materials and I can afford that from my savings. If I remember, there are tins of paint in the cellar left from last time. There might be enough to at least do one room.

Decision made. I'll begin on the bedrooms. And what better time than the present?

Fired with new enthusiasm, I jump to my feet. Not a wise move. As the room sways slightly, I suspect I have over-imbibed, but things settle again and I head upstairs.

Which room shall I do first?

I go to the master bedroom. This room

really isn't that bad. I reckon one coat of paint will be sufficient to freshen it up.

Before I can paint I'll have to get the dust sheets from the attic, but I'll do that tomorrow. What I can do now is move the furniture into the middle of the room. That shouldn't be difficult.

I move some of the smaller pieces, then stoop to tackle the bed. As I bend down to push, I feel my head swim.

I really shouldn't have had that second glass — or was it a third? I'm not too sure and I have a horrible feeling I'm going to regret it in the morning.

Ignoring my aching head, I shove the bed into the centre of the room, then the chest of drawers. I pile the small items like chairs and bedside tables on top of the bed.

This is easy. At this rate I'll be ready to start painting in the morning.

That just leaves the wardrobe. It's big and unwieldy but it's empty so shouldn't be too heavy. Anyway, I've moved it many times before in order to clean.

Carefully I swivel it round corner by

corner, walking it gradually towards the centre of the room. Then the back leg gets caught in the carpet and refuses to budge.

Perhaps I should wait until someone can help, but I'm on a roll now and want to get the job finished, so I give it a hefty push.

The top tilts and rocks and I only just manage to jump out of the way before the whole darned thing crashes to the floor with a terrific thump.

I fall backwards against the bed and slide to the floor next to the offending wardrobe, my heart leaping like a yo-yo at several 100 beats a second.

I'm wondering how on earth I'm going to get the wardrobe upright again when the door flies open and Max rushes in.

'What the hell is going on?' He glances around, taking in the chaos.

'What does it look like?' I retort, still flat on my back on the floor. 'And what are you doing here, anyway?'

'Never mind that. What are you doing?'

'I'd have thought that was obvious.

I'm moving furniture.'

'Do you want to tell me why?'

'Not particularly.'

From the look on his face, I deduce that is not the right answer.

'Because I'm going to paint the walls tomorrow,' I concede.

'And what gave you that idiotic idea?'

'It has to be done. The bank tells me I have no money to pay someone to do it for me. So I have to DIY it.

'I've done it before, you know. It's easy. Nothing to it.'

He sighs.

'You really are the most exasperating woman. You're extremely lucky you weren't hurt.'

'Nope,' I say, feeling around. 'All in one piece. No bones broken.'

I suddenly realise how I must look, lying down here on the floor, and I sit up quickly. Big mistake. My head swims and I groan out loud.

In a second, Max is beside me.

'It's OK,' I hasten to assure him. 'I'm fine. Just a bit of a headache.'

'You've been drinking,' he says.

Gosh, are the fumes that bad?

'Not only are you moving heavy furniture while you're alone in the house, with no-one to help if you have an accident, but you are doing it in a state of semi-inebriation.'

'What do you expect me to do? Sit around waiting for someone to do it for me? I'm not helpless, you know.'

'Just foolhardy. I'd expect you at least to wait until you're sober.'

'You would, would you?'

'Yes, I would. Supposing you'd ended up underneath the wardrobe? What would you have done?'

'Called for help.'

'Don't be ridiculous. Have some common sense, for heaven's sake!'

'Don't shout at me,' I yell.

Suddenly, I've had enough. My chest is tight and my eyes are stinging and if he says one more word, I think I'll burst into tears.

'This is my house and if I want to move things around, I will. I'll paint the whole house purple if I feel like it! And you can't stop me.'

I can hold back the tears no longer. Max presses a handkerchief into my hand, then puts his arms round me and holds me while I cry into his jacket.

I must still be under the influence because it feels surprisingly good. After all that has happened over the past weeks, that I've been bottling up inside me, it's such a relief to let it out.

I rest my face against his shoulder and sob noisily.

When eventually I begin to feel calmer and the sobs subside, the reality of the situation hits me as I realise where I am. And I like it.

Max is holding me close and I'm acutely aware of his head resting against mine, his warm breath on my cheek and his arms wrapped round me. I feel warm and comfortable and safe and I could happily stay here for ever.

'Feeling better?' Max's voice is gentle and caring.

I nod and wish I hadn't.

'Ouch!'

'Painful, eh?'

'You could say that.'

He sits me up and holds me at arms' length. Our eyes meet and it's as if I've touched a live wire as my whole body zings with a jolt of electricity.

I think he feels it, too, because just for a moment there's a tense silence between us. Then my leg gets cramp and I look away and the spell is broken.

'When did you last eat?' he asks.

I'm not sure. I have a feeling it might have been breakfast. No wonder the wine went to my head!

'This morning, I think.'

'You need food. Go and freshen up while I go and investigate your fridge.'

'You can be awfully bossy sometimes, you know,' I tell him.

'So I've been told. I'll see you in the kitchen in half an hour.'

I sit for a moment after he's left the room, wondering if I've misjudged him. My head, despite its delicate condition, is telling me to be careful, but my heart is telling me something very different.

I wash my face, brush my hair and apply a dash of make-up. Not too much. I don't want him thinking I'm making an effort for his sake. Just enough to make me feel better.

Then I go downstairs to see what kind of mess he's making of my kitchen and I'm met with a delicious aroma of garlic and mushrooms. Goodness, can the man cook as well?

Looking completely at home, with one of Molly's flowery pinnies tied round his waist, Max is breaking eggs expertly into a bowl. Sliced mushrooms are cooking gently in the frying pan and I smell garlic bread warming in the oven.

His suit jacket is hanging with his tie over the back of one of the chairs. He's rolled up his shirt sleeves and loosened his collar and, even in the girly pinny, he looks drop-dead gorgeous.

He's not doing my pulse rate any good at all.

He looks up and smiles.

'How does mushroom omelette and

garlic bread sound?'

'Wonderful.'

I watch in admiration as he whisks the eggs and tips them into the pan with the mushrooms and produces a perfect omelette.

'By the way,' I say, 'do you mind telling me how you managed to get into the house?'

'It wasn't difficult. You shouldn't go around leaving doors unlocked.'

'I don't, as a rule. I guess I had other things on my mind when I came home.'

'I hope you'll be more careful in future.'

As I open my mouth to protest, he cuts in.

'Omelette's ready.'

He halves the omelette and tips it on to two plates. I quickly lay the table with mats and cutlery while he takes the garlic bread from the oven.

'Should I offer you a glass of wine,' I ask, 'or are you driving?'

'As you have probably had enough for both of us, perhaps we should stick to water?'

I start to tell him if I want a drink I will have one, but change my mind and say nothing. For some reason, I don't want to spoil the evening.

Anyway, he's right. I have had more than enough.

The food is delicious and we finish off with fresh fruit and coffee.

'That was a lovely meal,' I say with a sigh of contentment. 'You should come more often,' I add without thinking.

It's just one of those throw-away phrases you say without meaning it, but it's too late to take it back.

'Thank you. I will be happy to take you up on your invitation.'

He laughs.

'Don't worry, I know you didn't mean it literally.'

Actually, I think I might have done.

Max leans back in his chair and stretches.

'Feeling better?'

'Much. I don't expect you to believe it, but I don't make a habit of drinking

110

alone. It's just that it's been a particularly bad day and, well . . .' I shrug. 'Enough said.'

'Do you want to talk about it?'

Do I? It can't do any harm as he probably knows most of it anyway.

'Where do I start?'

'How about the beginning?'

So I do. It takes a while and another pot of coffee.

'The way I see it,' I say after I've told him everything, 'is that we have a whole lot of questions and no answers. For a start, why did Dad need to come to you for help?

'Why did he allow the business to go downhill so quickly? Why is there no money in the bank?

'Why did he pay out such large amounts in the last week of his life? And to whom?

'And, what I find most puzzling of all, why didn't he contact me? Also, I've been thinking about the accident. Dad was a good driver. He didn't take risks.

'Empty road, fine weather, yet something made him lose control and drive into a tree. Don't you think that's really strange?'

'There could be a perfectly reasonable explanation for any of these in isolation, but I'm inclined to agree with you. When you put it all together, it does make you wonder.'

'The visit to the bank finished me. To be told there's no money in the account and no chance of a loan without income or a deposit was the final straw.'

'Then we need to find solutions.'

'Just like that? I suppose you can make miracles as easily as you make omelettes?'

'Unfortunately, no.'

'Max, do you know Giles Mason? He owns the Mermaid at the harbour.'

He shakes his head.

'Not that I recall.'

'He's a friend of Dad's. I went to see him the other day, thinking he might give me advice on renovating the old stables.'

'And did he?'

'No. He was against the whole idea.

Told me it was too much for me to take on. Also, I mentioned you and his reaction was quite odd.'

Max frowns.

'In what way?'

'He warned me not to trust you.'

I tell him what Giles said about him taking over failing businesses.

'He seemed to think you might have your eye on the Folly.'

Max's expression darkens.

'Why would he think that? You say this man is a friend?'

'Of Dad's, yes.'

He thinks for a moment then shrugs.

'Forget it for now. Let's talk about this idea you have for riding holidays.'

'You don't like it?'

'Actually, I do. I think it's a good one.'

'Oh!'

I'm surprised. I'd expected him to rubbish it.

'In fact, I wonder you didn't do it years ago, before the buildings became so dilapidated.'

'You really think it's workable?' I'm

beginning to feel excited. 'Emma and I had a good look round yesterday and we know what we're needing to do and how we can run it.

'We realise there's a lot of work needed on the stables and that's why I went to the bank to try to get funding.'

I make a gesture of exasperation.

'And here we are, back at the big stumbling block. Money.'

'There are ways I can help you.'

I put my hands up.

'Stop right there. I haven't changed my mind about that. I know you're not short of a penny or two, but I won't let you pay for it.

'I said I'll do it alone and I will. I owe you more than enough without adding to the debt.'

'Just how do you think you're going to achieve anything without money?'

'I'll find it from somewhere.'

'Where?'

Good question.

'I have some savings of my own,' I tell him. 'And there's Dad's life insurance.

'All I have to do is wait for probate to go through and I'm sure I can survive until then.'

Max leans back in his chair looking at me, an exasperated expression on his face.

'Even if you get a good insurance payout, do you have any idea how much it will cost to repair those stables and get the house up to a standard where you can charge guests enough to be able to recoup your investment?'

I shrug.

'I'll be able to get a bank loan by then.'

'So you'll still be adding to your debt, even though it won't be to me.

'And you still won't have an income to enable you to make repayments. The bank will want some kind of security.'

'I'll use the house as collateral.'

'What if it goes wrong? You stand to lose the house as well.'

Oh, he's impossible.

'Why are you determined to find problems?' I demand. 'If I do nothing, I'll lose the house anyway.

'Besides, you never know. Difficult though you might find it to believe, I might actually manage to make a success of it.'

Still, annoyingly, I know he's right.

The thing is, no doubt Max will have plenty of good ideas, but his business experience is in upmarket hotels for upmarket clients, mostly situated in urban areas.

Probably the nearest any of them get to countryside is a few windowboxes or a perfectly manicured garden.

What the Folly offers is almost the complete opposite.

'May I point out,' I say, 'you may be a Mr Big in your own area of expertise, but what does a city man like you know about the kind of people who come to a rural area like this?

'Or the kind of holiday experience they are looking for? You and I cater for a completely different kind of visitor.'

He says nothing for a moment. Then he nods slowly.

'You may have a point. I agree my

expertise is in a different type of hotel, and I do spend most of my time working with high-powered businessmen and wealthy clients.

'So, what do you suggest we do about it?'

That throws me. I didn't expect him to agree with me.

'You need to get to know the kind of people we cater for.'

'OK. Perhaps you should arrange for me to meet some of these country people?'

I have a crazy thought. I don't know what makes me say it (perhaps the drink hasn't worn off yet) but the words are out before I can stop them.

'Come to the barn dance,' I challenge. 'The whole village will be there and there couldn't be a better way of experiencing country life and meeting people.'

He won't agree, surely. To my amazement he does.

'That sounds like a good idea. When is it?'

I'm completely taken aback. Somehow

I can't picture this suave entrepreneur in his hand tailored suit, letting his hair down in a muddy marquee, downing pints of scrumpy with the locals.

He'll stand out like a sore thumb.

But I've issued the challenge and I'll have to stand by it.

'It's tomorrow.'

'Good, I'm free. I shall look forward to it.'

He grins and I'm sure he knows I'm regretting my hasty invitation.

I'm lost for words. What have I let myself in for?

The Barn Dance

My eyes open the following morning to find another glorious day. Rather than spend it in the office, I ride Freddy out towards Dunkery.

After the emotional upheaval of the previous evening, I need something to clear my head and get me back on an even keel.

I wish I could work out what I feel about Max.

One minute I see him as the enemy, interfering and trying to take over. The next, I'm dreaming of his arms round me and my head resting on his shoulder.

I'm still unsure what part he's played in the mystery of Dad's last weeks and until I know that, I still can't quite trust him.

I thrust him to the back of my mind. There's nothing like a ride over the moor to put life into perspective and by the time I take Freddy back to his field, two hours later, I'm relaxed and at one with the world.

I find Emma has brought Monty back and the two ponies greet each other with affectionate nipping and play-fighting, happy to be together again.

I go to the office to check the post and find Clare busy sorting papers.

'Hi.' I drop my helmet on a chair and shrug off my jacket. 'I didn't expect to see you today. It's not one of your days.'

'I know, but there's so much to do I thought I'd come in for a while.'

'Thanks. I appreciate it.'

I sit down, pull off my boots and stretch my legs.

'Heavens, I'm out of practice. Either that or I'm feeling the effects of last night.'

I realise my mistake as soon as the words are out of my mouth.

Clare looks up, instantly alert.

'Oh? And what happened last night?' She'll only badger me until I tell, so I fill her in without going into too much detail.

She rolls her eyes.

'You wicked woman,' she jokes. 'I am so jealous. That is one sexy man.'

'Don't read anything into it. Just because we spent an amicable hour or so together doesn't mean we are bosom buddies.'

Clare gives me a look and I pull a face.

'Trust me. Nothing happened'

'You should bring him to the barn dance.'

She's joking, I think, but I know my face has turned scarlet.

'You're not!' she exclaims. 'You dark horse. I thought you couldn't stand him?'

'It's a business arrangement,' I tell her.

'Pull the other one.'

I'm not going to rise to it.

'I'm going to get changed,' I tell her. 'I'll see you later.'

★ ★ ★

I can't deny I'm looking forward to the barn dance, but I'm also feeling nervous.

I'm not sure if it's the thought of spending the evening with Max or the

121

thought of having to introduce him to everyone and put up with the good-natured ragging I know I shall get.

I can't decide if he will fit in with the crowd or stand out like a sore thumb.

I stand in the shower, enjoying the sensuous feel of warm water running through my hair and down my back, and try to decide what to wear.

It's an ordinary village event and people are pretty casual in the way they dress for it. I've always worn jeans and a checked shirt but maybe I should make more of an effort this year.

Something a bit more feminine. A skirt, perhaps, and boots.

I wonder what Max will wear.

I rinse the conditioner from my hair and step out of the shower.

What am I thinking about? It's only Max. He's not a boyfriend or anyone particularly special and this certainly isn't a date.

As I told Clare, it's a business meeting to introduce him to the kind of people who might stay at the Folly. I'll do well to remember that, I tell myself sternly.

I decide there is no need to make a special effort and I'll wear jeans as usual.

I was given a bottle of perfume as a leaving present by my Australian hosts and I squirt a little behind my ears. Then I give another little squirt down the front of my shirt for good measure.

Hair up or down? Down, I decide. It's one of my better features so I might as well make the most of it.

I'm studying the effect in the mirror, hoping I haven't overdone the perfume, when I hear his car on the gravel. Seconds later the bell rings.

I give my appearance a quick once-over, decide it will do and make my way downstairs.

I open the door and do a double-take. Is this the suave man-in-a-suit who has been the bane of my life for the past few days?

He's dressed in jeans, cowboy-style boots and a denim shirt, open at the neck and showing just the right amount of extremely sexy chest. It's having a very unsettling effect on my equilibrium.

'Not too early, am I?' he asks.

I swallow; finally my mouth starts working.

'Er, no. I'm just about ready.'

'Good. Shall we go?'

Making an effort to regain control of my senses, I take a torch from the hall table and drop it into my bag.

We'll need it in the pitch darkness that will have fallen by the time we come home.

My pulse quickens at the thought of walking back in the dark with Max.

I push the thought away and pick up my jacket. He takes it and holds it out for me to put on. As I shrug into it, his hand brushes my neck and a shiver runs down me.

I remind myself this is business. There is nothing personal here at all.

The trouble is, I don't really believe it.

'Do we walk or drive?'

'It's only down the combe to the village. We walk.'

It's already that half light that comes at

dusk. Across the bay, the sun is hovering above the cliffs in a blaze of red against the blackening sky, sending shadows playing through the trees and painting the autumn leaves with shades of gold.

Evenings like this always stir my emotions but this evening the feeling is more intense than usual. I wonder if Max feels it, too, as he's making no attempt at conversation.

The silence between us is comfortable and I determine to put worries behind me and enjoy the evening.

I wonder what the reaction will be when I walk in with him. It will certainly cause a stir, and not only because he's an outsider.

Halfway down the combe we can already hear the sound of voices and music playing.

I turn to Max.

'Are you sure you are ready for this?'

'I wouldn't miss it.'

'Just remember, you asked to come.'

He grins.

'Actually, I didn't. But stop worrying.

Come on. Let's join the party.'

We walk into the marquee and immediately I feel everyone looking at us. Any stranger would spark interest but Max is no ordinary stranger and in minutes we are surrounded by curious women.

'Who have we here?'

Trust Marge Penn to be first in line. She runs the village shop and post office, keeping the village supplied with gossip and flirting with every man she meets.

'You're a dark horse, Jessica Flynn,' she says with a big grin. 'Where have you been hiding this gorgeous man?'

She places her hand on Max's arm.

'I'll claim a dance from you later, my lovely.'

I feel my cheeks burn with embarrassment.

Max comes to my rescue.

'How can I refuse an offer like that?' he answers with a smile. 'I shall be delighted.'

Marge flutters her eyelashes, overcome by his gallantry.

'I'll be waiting for 'ee.'

Max grins at me as she moves away.

'I can see this is going to be a fun evening,' he whispers.

I spend the next quarter of an hour introducing him to everyone. To my surprise, he seems completely at home.

Eventually we make it to the bar for a drink and, as the music begins, everyone's attention turns to the dancing.

It's the usual village ensemble: Fred Webber with his fiddle and Saul Rook with his accordion. Matthew Hall, the vicar, is doing a great job as caller.

It's good to be home again and getting back into village life. Just like old times. My only regret is Dad isn't here to enjoy it.

I see Clare come in with Emma and Bill. They sit at a table over the far side of the marquee and, deciding there is safety in numbers, I take Max over to meet them.

'Hi. Mind if we join you?'

Clare immediately moves along.

'Are you kidding?' she asks, patting the seat beside her. 'Where did you find this handsome stranger?'

'Clare!' I exclaim, vowing to kill her later. 'Behave yourself. You know perfectly well who this is. Max, meet my bookkeeper and, very possibly ex-friend Clare.

'And this is Emma, whom I have told you about, and her husband, Bill.'

Max takes the offered seat next to Clare and I squeeze between Bill and Emma.

I'm surprised how easily Max is fitting in. While I catch up with Emma he talks to Bill about farming and horses as if he was a farmer himself. Is there no end to his talents?

Dave Cook, from Marsh Farm, comes across and asks Clare to dance. I can see she is torn between accepting and staying with Max but eventually she goes with Dave.

Bill and Emma join them. Max stands up.

'Shall we?'

'You dance?' I'm surprised.

'Why don't we find out?'

128

He takes my hand and I feel that same spark again as he leads me on to the floor and we take our place among the dancers.

I've never really registered before how physical barn dancing is, but right now I'm aware of Max's arm round my shoulders and my hands in his. It's not only the act of dancing that is making my heart pound.

He certainly can dance. I've been to many village barn dances over the years but I've never enjoyed one as much as this.

Of course, everyone assumes he is my boyfriend and we are getting a fair amount of good-natured teasing, but Max takes it all in his stride and even seems to enjoy it.

True to his promise, he partners Marge and her friend in the Dashing White Sergeant while I sit and get my breath back.

I find myself wondering how I could ever have disliked him. Maybe it's something to do with the atmosphere this evening.

It's pitch dark outside now and the

lighting inside the marquee is subdued, so, despite the adrenaline-fuelled music and dancing, it feels like being in a romantic cocoon where the outside world is a whole other place, somewhere it can't touch me.

The hours pass so quickly. In hardly any time at all, the evening is drawing to a close and I realise I don't want it to end.

The vicar calls the last dance and Max and I join everyone else on the floor. The dance is the Rosza, one of my favourites.

It's slow compared to most of the other dances and it's danced as couples rather than in circles or squares, so it's a lovely romantic one to end with.

Strange, I've never thought of it as being romantic before.

Max takes my hands and we stand face to face, swaying in time to the music. Then he lifts his arm for me to make a half turn underneath it.

My back is tight against his chest and his arms are clasping mine across my ribs as we continue to sway. He swings me round again to take us into a waltz.

Then I'm facing him again before turning under his arm and relaxing into him, my spine against his chest and his arms holding me close.

I lose count of how many times we repeat the moves. All I am aware of, when the music finally stops, is of being held tight against him as he tilts my face up to his and oh, so slowly, his lips come down to touch mine and the world stops turning for several seconds.

'Jessica,' he murmurs when we come up for air. 'I think it's time I took you home.'

I'm not about to argue.

We collect our jackets and leave the marquee, calling goodbyes as we go.

Together, we make our way up the combe by torchlight. Somewhere an owl hoots and is answered by its mate. Bats flit through the darkness, searching for prey.

The night sky is brilliant with stars. It's a perfect end to a perfect evening.

Village Talk

Clare is in the kitchen making coffee when I go downstairs the following morning.

'My, you are keen,' I tease. 'I thought you'd be having a lie-in after last night. Don't you have any other work to go to?'

'Not today. I want to hear all the news.'

I pretend not to understand.

'What news would that be?'

'Come on, don't keep me in suspense. What happened last night?'

I take some bread out of the bin and begin making toast.

'Gosh, I'm hungry,' I say.

It's true, I am hungry, but I can't resist teasing Clare.

'Don't be mean, Jessica Flynn. Come on, tell all.'

The toast pops up.

'Actually . . .' I pause.

'Yes?'

'Max walked me home. It was such a beautiful evening. We sat on the terrace for a while looking at the moonlight on the sea.'

I rummage in the drawer for a knife and take my time getting butter and marmalade from the cupboard.

I can feel Clare scowling at me.

'Jess . . .'

'Then he put his arms round me.' I start spreading butter, slowly.

'And then?'

'Then he kissed me. And then . . .'

'Yes?'

'He went home and I went to bed.'

Clare's face is a picture.

'Honestly? Is that all?''

'Honestly, that's all. I'm sorry I don't have lots of raunchy details for you but that's how it was. I stayed. He went.'

'Oh. Well, never mind. It's obvious he likes you and I'd say the feeling is mutual.

'So he'll be in touch again pretty soon. Believe me.'

'I doubt it. The way everyone was all over him, I bet he regrets getting involved.

'He's probably looking to let me down gently and revert to a purely business footing.'

'Don't you believe it. I saw the way he was looking at you all evening. In fact, the whole village did.

'Marge will have you engaged by now. I bet you're both the talk of the post office this morning.'

I groan.

'What a horrible thought.'

Marge is an incorrigible busybody and there's nothing she enjoys more than an audience and a good gossip.

'You'll see. By tomorrow she'll have you walking up the aisle.'

'She'll be disappointed. Whatever else develops between Max and me, it certainly won't include that sort of relationship.'

I'm not admitting, even to Clare, that I thought of little else lying in bed last night, unable to sleep for thinking about him.

I spread marmalade on my cold toast and take a bite just as the phone rings.

I gesture to Clare to answer it. Despite what I said, part of me hopes it'll be Max.

Clare passes the phone to me.

'It's Emma.'

I swallow the toast in my mouth and take the phone.

'Hi, Emma. How are you this morning?'

'Fine, thanks. Brilliant evening, wasn't it? How about you?'

I laugh.

'I suppose you're dying to know how I got on with Max? Clare was here at the crack of dawn, giving me the third degree.'

Emma chuckles.

'Well, how did it go?'

'As I told Clare, we walked back. We talked a while. He went home. And that was all.

'I'm sorry to disappoint you.'

'Never mind. Give him time. Actually I wondered when you wanted to have another look at the stables.

'I can be free tomorrow, if that's any good?'

'Great. Why don't you come for coffee? There are things I must do today anyway.'

'Sounds good. See you then.'

* * *

I don't hear from Max, despite Clare's prophecy, and I admit I'm disappointed. After last night, I expected at least a phone call.

But, then, why should he? He has a hotel chain to run and he warned me when we first met he wouldn't be able to spend much time at the Folly.

I busy myself doing much-needed housework. Not my favourite occupation, but I can't expect Molly to do it all.

By lunchtime I'm aching all over, but the first-floor rooms are clean and tidy and there are just two that really do need a coat of paint.

The others will do as they are, for the time being, at least.

Molly and I eat a quick lunch of soup and bread and cheese, then I walk down to the village.

I want to find Jim Rudd, our local

handyman, to ask if he is free to do the painting and help with work on the stables.

Also, I need to go to the post office to buy stamps and post letters for Clare. It's something I'm not looking forward to as Marge is sure to have plenty to say after the events of last night.

I'm right. The minute I walk in, she looks up from serving a customer and her face splits into a beaming smile.

'Hello, my lovely!' she calls. 'And how are you this afternoon?'

'I'm fine, thank you, Marge.'

'And that handsome young man of yours? How is he today?'

I seethe inwardly.

'I really wouldn't know, Marge. And he's not my young man; just a business acquaintance.'

'I don't know about that. The way he were looking at you at that barn dance, I think the acquaintance he had in mind were more than just a business one.'

I bite my lip and remain silent while Marge finishes serving her customer.

Then she turns back to me.

'Now, what can I get you, my lovely?'

'A book of first-class stamps, please, Marge,' I say, hoping she's finished making comments.

There aren't many people in the shop but I can tell from the silence they are listening to every word and taking it all in.

'How are things at the Folly?' Marge asks. 'Getting sorted now, are you?'

'Pretty good, thank you.' I start sticking stamps on Clare's letters.

'It do seem strange not having Sam round the village,' Marge continues. 'And strange for you, too, of course, not having him round the house.'

'Yes, it is.'

I smile at her. She might be a gossip but she's well meaning and has a kind heart.

'It does seem empty but I'm slowly getting used to him not being there.'

'Well, if there's anything I can do to help, you just let me know.'

'Thank you, Marge, that's kind of you.

Now, I need to find Jim Rudd and see if he can do some painting for me.'

'He were doing some work in the orchard this morning. You might find him still there.'

I thank her again, pick up the unused stamps and go outside to drop the letters in the postbox.

I stroll through the village towards the community orchard, where I find Jim busy collecting windfalls.

He's the first port of call for everyone in the village when they have odd jobs.

As an ex-builder, he can turn his hand to just about anything.

He retired several years ago but still works when he feels like it to supplement his pension.

I explain what I want and he immediately agrees.

'You caught me at the right time,' he says. 'I've nothing much on at the moment so I can come up later, if you like, and see what needs doing.'

'Thanks, Jim. I'm heading back now so any time you're ready, I'll be there.'

139

'Right you are.'

We chat a few moments longer, then I say goodbye and make my way home.

Clare has left, so I make a cup of tea and curl up in front of the Aga to read for a while until Jim arrives.

Maybe I'll sort Dad's room tomorrow. I'm pretty sure there will be things in his private desk that Simon needs to have.

It's warm in front of the Aga and I find myself nodding over the book and my eyes closing. I must have gone to sleep because I wake with a start to hear knocking at the door and Jim's voice calling me.

Rubbing the sleep from my eyes I let him in. I show him the two rooms I've earmarked for painting.

'I'll move the furniture and put covers on,' I tell him. 'I need to keep the cost as low as possible. What do you think?'

'Shouldn't be difficult,' he says. 'I reckon if you do that, and the cleaning up afterwards, I could get it done in a couple of days.

'If you're not wanting any fancy colours, I know where I can get hold of some magnolia paint cheap, or plain white if you'd rather.'

We settle for white.

'So, plus two days labour, that would come to . . .' He does a quick mental calculation and names a price.

'Perfect,' I agree.

'Right, I'll see you tomorrow afternoon, then, if that's OK?'

'Wonderful. Thanks, Jim.'

I see him out. At last I'm making progress. With a bit of luck, within a week I'll be open for business again.

Next time I see Clare I must talk to her about marketing and ask her to plan some adverts.

A Day Out

'Any news from you-know-who?' Clare asks when I see her the following day.

'No. And I'm not expecting any yet.'

As if on cue, at that moment the phone rings. Clare picks it up and her face breaks into a wide grin as she listens.

'Hold on a minute, please.' She passes me the phone, speaking in a stage whisper. 'It's him! I told you he'd call. And, guess what, he wants you to find him a horse.'

I glower at her, even though my pulse has gone into overdrive.

'What are you on about?'

'A horse. He wants a horse.'

'And is he offering me his kingdom?' I take the phone.

'My kingdom?' Max asks, clearly having heard. 'No, but how about a day out instead?'

'You heard?'

'How could I miss?'

I'm curious.

142

'What do you want a horse for? I didn't know you could ride.'

He chuckles.

'I'm full of surprises. Can you find me one this morning?'

'I can ask Emma, I suppose.'

'Good. Get that pony of yours saddled and I'll see you in an hour.'

'Hang on, supposing I don't want to?' But he's disconnected.

Although I'm not about to let Max know, the idea of a day out with him is appealing. Work on the stables will have to wait.

'Don't keep me in suspense,' Clare urges. 'What was all that about?'

Trying not to appear too excited, I fill her in, then phone Emma to organise a horse.

I'm waiting on the drive with Freddy when Max drives up. He climbs out of the Mercedes and my heart skips a beat.

What is it about this man that continually gets my adrenaline levels jumping? If it's not with anger or frustration, it's with an emotion I haven't yet quite identified.

Or, if I'm honest, maybe I have, but just don't want to acknowledge it.

If I'd thought the jeans he wore for the barn dance were sexy, they have nothing on the thigh-hugging jodhs he's wearing this morning. They, and the high boots that complete the effect, show evidence of much use and clearly aren't new.

It doesn't seem to matter what he's wearing — city suit, jeans, riding gear — he looks stunning in all of them.

He pulls a helmet from the passenger seat, closes the car door and walks across.

'Ready?'

'It would be nice to know what I'm ready for,' I reply.

'All in good time.' He looks around. 'Where is my mount?'

'Waiting for you at Emma's.'

He nods towards Freddy.

'I hope it's not one of those.'

'Don't be ridiculous. You are far too tall and heavy.'

He grins.

'Just joking. Let's go and find the horse.'

I lead Freddy and we walk down to Emma's yard on the edge of the village where her riding-school is based.

She has saddled up Titan, a 17-hand ex-hunter.

'I thought you might need something tall, with those long legs of yours,' she says to Max with a grin.

'Thanks a bunch, Emma.' I grimace.

Titan is a good 18 inches taller than Freddy, which will put me at a distinct disadvantage and, from his expression, I can see that Max has immediately picked up on it.

He swings easily into the saddle and looks down at me with a grin that says it all though, give him his due, he resists the temptation to make any sarcastic remarks.

'Have a good day,' Emma calls as we ride out.

'Right,' Max says. 'Let's go.'

We turn into the lane and head through the village to a bridleway leading up through a wooded combe and on to open moorland. In three directions the moor stretches as far as the eye can see.

Before us lies the sea, sparkling in the sunshine, and beyond that the Welsh coast and the outline of the Brecon Beacons.

'Are you going to tell me where we're going?' I ask.

'Nope.'

'Well, I hope you know the way, wherever it is.'

'Oh, I think I'll manage. Just follow me and enjoy the ride.'

Freddy has to work hard to keep up with Titan's long stride but Exmoors are tough and plucky and he gives me a wonderful ride, striding out to stay level with his big companion.

We head inland, past grazing sheep and groups of shaggy Highland cattle. Buzzards mew overhead, soaring the thermals and searching the ground for prey.

So far, Max hasn't made any reference to the evening of the barn dance, but there's a subtle change in our relationship today.

We're heading towards Exford. Maybe he's taking me for lunch at the White Horse, one of my favourite pubs.

But before we get there, he turns off the bridleway and heads downhill on a path I'm not familiar with, winding through ancient oak woodland.

The trees grow thin and tall as they reach for the light, and their straggly twisted branches drip with lichens of all kinds. Tree roots form great mossy mounds among the undergrowth of fern and wild flowers.

There are many such places on Exmoor and the sight never fails to move me. This is truly magical.

We emerge from the trees into open farmland. Max pulls up and indicates the farm buildings lower down the hill.

'Oakhanger.'

'Is that where we're going?'

'Yep.'

I'm intrigued.

We ride into the farmyard and halt outside an old pillared linhay. As we dismount a man emerges from a nearby barn.

'Max! Good to see you, but what brings you here? And who is this young lady?'

Max puts a hand on my arm.

'Jessica, meet my father, Hugh. Dad, this is Jessica Flynn.'

Hugh's face breaks into a wide smile.

'Of course! I knew there was something familiar about you — you're Sam's girl. It's good to see you again, Jessica.'

It's hard to believe Max Corrigan actually has such a mundane thing as a father.

'It's good to meet you, too, Mr Corrigan. But you said 'again'? I'm sorry, but I don't remember meeting you before.'

'I'm not surprised. You were about five years old last time I saw you!

'You were learning to ride a pony and, as I remember, spending as much time on the ground as in the saddle. I was most impressed by your determination.'

He glances at Freddy.

'Not this pony, I take it?'

'No, that would have been Monty. He's too old to trek across the moor now, much as he would love to.

'I'm afraid poor Monty had to put up with a lot of falling off in those days.'

'Well, I'm glad to see you finally learned to stay on.' He grins, then becomes serious. 'I was so sorry to hear about Sam.

'He'd been to see me some weeks before the accident and I left soon after to go abroad, which is why I couldn't get to the funeral.

'Max tried to reach me but unfortunately I was out of contact.'

'I understand, Mr Corrigan. I only just got back in time myself.'

'Did you enjoy your adventure in the outback?'

'Very much, but I'm glad to be back.'

'Now, you must both be hungry and thirsty if you've ridden from Larkcombe. Why don't you put the horses in the linhay? You'll find hay in there.

'Then come inside and I'll rustle up a drink and something to eat.'

As he walks away, I hiss at Max.

'Why did you let me think you were a city boy and all the time your father runs a farm? I won't forgive you for this.'

'Perhaps that will teach you not to jump to conclusions.' Max laughs.

'Were you born here?'

'No, you were right about me being a city boy. I was born in London.

'Dad bought this place after his first big business deal. I was about ten years old.'

'So you've lived here most of your life, then. More country than city.'

'You could say that. I certainly prefer the country life, believe it or not.'

'Is this still your home?'

'As often as it can be. I have an apartment in London which I use when I'm in town.

'Now, let's get these animals under cover and settled. I could eat a horse.'

'Shush!' I cover Freddy's ears with my hands. 'Not in front of Freddy and Titan.'

He bursts out laughing.

'How insensitive of me. I apologise.'

In great good humour we unsaddle them both, top up the water buckets and fill a couple of haynets.

'OK,' Max says. 'I'm starving. Let's eat.'

We go into a lovely old farmhouse kitchen where two collies amble over to say hello. I bend down to stroke them.

'Meet Jack and Jill,' Max says. 'Brother and sister.'

'And wonderful sheepdogs,' Hugh adds.

'Do you just farm sheep, Mr Corrigan?'

'Yes. Mostly Horn and Blue Face. But please call me Hugh. Sit yourselves down while I get some food.'

Max and I make ourselves comfortable on the settle, in front of a modern Aga built into the huge inglenook fireplace.

It's a beautiful room and, judging from the low beams and flagged floor, I guess this house is considerably older than the Folly.

I lean towards Max, enjoying the intimacy, enclosed between the settle's high back and the fireplace.

'Are you hiding a mother away somewhere, as well?' I ask quietly so his father won't hear. 'Planning to spring her on me later as another surprise?'

'My mother left some years ago. She couldn't stand the life here.'

I groan inwardly.

'Sorry,' I whisper.

'You see, you and I have more in common than you realise.'

Except you still have your father, I think.

Lunch is delicious — fresh home-baked bread with cheese and pickles, washed down with local cider. Culinary talent clearly runs in the family.

'Now,' Hugh says, when we have eaten, 'tell me why you have come to see me? I'm sure it isn't just to enjoy my company.'

'Jessica is looking for some answers and is hoping you can help,' Max tells him.

'It's about my father,' I explain. 'The accident, and some of his actions just before his death, don't make any sense to me.

'Max says you knew him well, so I

hoped you might be able to throw some light on what happened.'

'It's true we used to be close, but I hadn't seen Sam for years until he came to see me out of the blue a few weeks ago. It was quite a surprise, I have to say.'

'How was he? Was he in trouble, or ill?'

'He seemed a bit uneasy but I don't think he was ill, though he was complaining of a headache.

'He looked tired, too. Kept rubbing his eyes. Said he'd been working hard so I didn't think anything of it at the time.

'But I expect you are wondering about the power of attorney he drew up?'

I nod.

'Sam wanted me to have it in case he was unable to cope at any time. It's a common thing to do when you get to a certain age.

'It gives you security and peace of mind knowing someone will be able to deal with your affairs should anything happen to you. I didn't see anything odd about it.

'I did wonder why he chose me, mind

you, when he must have had other friends he could rely on for help.'

'That puzzles me, too,' I agree, thinking of Giles. 'There's a friend of his living close to us, whom he has known for years, yet he chose not to go to him. I wonder why.'

'Perhaps because I'd known him for so long and I've experience of running a business.'

'But that applies to this other friend, as well.'

Hugh shakes his head.

'Then I really don't know, Jessica. He must have had his reasons but we may never know what they were now.'

'I suppose. Why did you suggest he dealt with Max rather than you?'

'I spent most of my life building up the hotel chain, but when Max was old enough to take it over I decided to retire and become a full-time farmer.

'When Sam came to me I'd been out of touch for some years, and things move on. I suggested Max take it on instead, and Sam was quite happy with that.'

Well, that answered one question I'd had about Max. He had inherited the business from his father and it was Hugh who built Corrigan Enterprises.

Maybe Giles was wrong about Max and it was Hugh who had been the ruthless buyer-up of failing businesses. On the other hand, maybe it was neither of them.

Somehow I can't see either man being so heartless.

'It's as if he knew something was going to happen to him, isn't it?' I muse. 'Did he give any sign he was expecting anything?'

'Not really, though, as I say, he did seem uneasy. I tried to get him to open up but, whatever it was, he didn't want to talk about it.'

'Did you help set up the agreement?'

'As his proposed attorney that wouldn't have been right, so I suggested he saw his solicitor. In the end, he told me he did it on line and it was certified by a business colleague. All perfectly above board.'

'I'm sure it was.'

But why hadn't Dad asked Simon?

'If I think of anything else, I'll contact you,' Hugh says. 'And if there is anything I can do to help, you must let me know.'

We remain at the table chatting. Hugh talks a lot about Dad.

I like him very much and find myself daydreaming of a future with an older Max who's a lot like his father.

I could happily stay here all day, listening to Hugh's stories of the past and just enjoying being near Max, but we still have to ride back across the moor before dark.

Regretfully, I say goodbye to Hugh and we mount the horses and make our way back to Larkcombe.

It has been the most extraordinary day. I'm no nearer understanding what happened to Dad but I am beginning to trust Max and see him as a friend.

By the time we return Titan to Emma and put Freddy back in his field, it's almost dark. We walk up the drive to where Max left his car and I wonder if I should invite him in for coffee, or something stronger, maybe. It seems a shame to end the day so soon with the evening still ahead of us.

But he clearly has other plans, because he makes straight for the car, opens the door and drops his helmet on the passenger seat. 'Are you off, then?' I ask, trying not to show my disappointment.

I'm sure he hesitates a fraction of a second before answering.

'I have to go, I'm afraid. Much as I would like to stay, there are things I must attend to.'

I shrug, attempting to be casual.

'No problem. I have loads to do, as well.'

'I hope you've enjoyed the day.'

'It's been wonderful. Thank you.'

'I think you were a hit with Dad.'

'I liked him, too.'

There's a long pause. Perhaps he doesn't want to leave yet.

'I must go,' he says at last.

He puts his hands on my shoulders and looks down at me.

'Take care, Jessica. And promise me, no more furniture moving if you are alone in the house!'

'I promise.'

'Good.'

He leans forward and I close my eyes in expectation. After what feels like hours but is probably a mere fraction of a second, his lips touch mine, and linger, sending shivers down my spine.

Too soon, he lifts his head and gently touches my lips with his finger.

'I have to go,' he murmurs. 'I'll see you soon.'

I watch as the Mercedes purrs down the drive, then I go in to the house still reeling from his touch. I've never felt this way about anyone before.

Is it possible I'm falling in love? With Max, of all people?

In a daze, I go to the kitchen wondering what I fancy for supper, my mind lingering on the memory of Max's kiss.

Only half concentrating, I flick through the post Clare has left on the table. She has also left a note.

Hi, Jess.

Tried to ring you but no signal. Can you contact Simon tomorrow ASAP? He says it's urgent. Clare.

My happy mood fizzles and dies and I come to earth with a bump. It must be bad news or she wouldn't have left a note like that.

If it was good news, she would have said what it was or waited until tomorrow to tell me.

After the highly charged emotional day with Max, it's too much. I give up the idea of supper. I was hungry but now the thought of food chokes me.

I sink into a chair and wonder what on earth Simon could want to see me about that is so important.

Unwelcome News

It's too late to call Simon now; he'll have left the office long ago. I'll just have to sleep on it. Though how much sleep I'll get is anyone's guess.

Perhaps if I read for a while I'll get tired enough to drop off, but first I need a hot bath. After the riding I've done today, I'll regret it in the morning if I don't have a soak now.

I go to the bathroom, turn on the hot tap and add calming lavender bath oil, then slide down into the warm perfumed water, close my eyes and let the bath work its magic.

Is it really only a few hours ago I came home from my day out with Max?

Meeting Hugh Corrigan has been a revelation. He's such a lovely man, no wonder Dad went to him for help.

I'm seeing Max differently, too. No longer as the enemy but as a friend.

I begin to feel calmer. Max won't let anything jeopardise the Folly. Of course he won't. He has too big a stake in it himself.

With that comforting thought, I start to unwind. My eyes grow heavy and begin to close.

I wake with a start to find the water has cooled. I climb out, towel myself dry and put on pyjamas, then climb into bed and pick up my book to read for a while.

The bath has helped. Whatever is waiting for me at the solicitor's tomorrow, I can deal with it. With Max's help.

* * *

When I wake the following morning the worry of Simon's phone call returns. As soon as his office opens I dial his number and arrange to go in straight away.

I contemplate calling on Isobel on my way out, but it isn't fair to involve her until I know more.

I drive into town, trying to keep my mind on the road and not let my concentration wander, but it's not easy with all kinds of worrying scenarios running

161

though my head.

Simon is in reception when I arrive.

'Jessica,' he says, 'come in.'

We go to his office. He gestures me towards a seat and settles himself behind his desk.

'Thank you for coming so quickly.'

'Please tell me what it is, Simon. I've been imagining all sorts of awful possibilities.'

'I'm afraid it isn't good news.'

He picks up a letter from his desk.

'I had this yesterday from Sam's insurance company.'

'Isn't that good news, if the insurance is finally coming through?'

'That's the problem. I'm afraid it isn't.'

He takes a deep breath as if he's not sure how to begin.

'It appears,' he says eventually, 'that your father omitted to inform the insurance company of something.'

My adrenaline level leaps. Is this what was worrying Dad?

'Please, Simon, just tell me. I can't bear the suspense.'

He sighs.

'Sam was having trouble with his eyesight. He had been diagnosed with AMD.'

Whatever I had been expecting, it isn't this.

'AMD? That's age-related something . . .' My mind goes blank.

'Macular degeneration.' Simon nods.

'I'm pretty sure there was nothing wrong with his sight when I left for Australia. Doesn't AMD develop over a long time?'

'Usually, yes, but Sam had a type that can develop over a matter of months.'

I think of my dad coping with the shock of losing his sight and no-one here to share it with. He must have been so worried!

No wonder some of his behaviour had been strange and out of character.

'How does that affect the insurance, Simon? Are you saying he wasn't covered?'

'Not exactly. But he should have told the insurance company and also the DVLC, because it can affect driving.

Apparently, his sight had deteriorated to the point where he shouldn't have been driving at all.'

'Oh!' The implications suddenly hit me. 'The crash. That's why he drove off the road. Because he couldn't see properly!'

'It's possible, yes.'

'He must have been so worried about everything and had so much on his mind, that perhaps he wasn't concentrating properly, either.'

'As I say, it's possible, but the bottom line is the insurance company is refusing to pay out because of this. Failure to declare the AMD means the insurance is invalidated.'

'Nothing at all?'

This is worse than I'd imagined. I'd been banking on that insurance money.

'I'm afraid so. I shall do my best to persuade them to pay you something, but I can't promise I'll be successful.'

'No, I understand.'

What do I do now? There are probably lots of questions I should be asking but I can't think straight.

I pick up my bag and stand up.

'Thank you, Simon. I must go.'

He comes round and takes my hands.

'Are you sure you're all right to drive home?' he asks.

'Yes. I'll be fine. Please don't worry.'

'Look, go and think things through and we can talk again when you've had a chance to assimilate it all. Meanwhile, I'll see what I can pull out of the bag.'

He opens the door for me.

'Take care, Jessica, and try not to worry too much. I'll be in touch.'

I give him a wobbly smile and head out of the building to find my car.

I climb into the driver's seat and pull out my mobile to phone Max. I punch in his number and wait while it rings, but it clicks on to voicemail. I suppose he's in a meeting, or driving.

I'm surprised at how much I want to speak to him and tell him about Dad. I drop the phone on to the passenger seat and start the car.

I'll go home and try again later.

A Trouble Shared

I drive in a daze, thinking how Dad must have felt, finding out he was losing his sight. No wonder he had the accident.

But it makes it even more inexplicable that he should be driving that day when he was clearly unfit to do so.

I can think of only one reason he would be driving along that particular road. To see Giles. So what was so important he felt it was worth the risk?

Back at the Folly I park in the yard and am about to try ringing Max again when Isobel calls to me from the Lodge.

I put the phone away and walk across to meet her, wondering what to tell her. She has a right to know, as it affects her as well.

As I get closer, I can see she realises something is wrong.

'What's happened, Jessica? You look dreadful.'

I grimace.

'More bad news, I'm afraid.'

166

'Come inside and tell me about it.'

I follow her into the kitchen. She reaches for the kettle then changes her mind.

'Not tea,' she says. 'You look as if something stronger is called for.'

'Isobel, it's the middle of the day!'

'There are some occasions when time is irrelevant. This may be one of them.'

She takes a bottle of Chardonnay from the fridge and pours us both a large glass.

I remember the last time I drowned bad news with a glass or two of wine. I must make sure I don't make a habit of this!

Isobel picks up the glasses.

'Let's sit by the fire.'

Sitting on the sofa, with Isobel in the chair beside me, I realise anew how pleased I am she's here. I never gave myself a chance to get to know her properly before.

She was always a distant and severe great-aunt to whom I was never able to get close.

It's amazing how that has changed

since the funeral. She's a lovely person and, despite the sixty or so years' difference in our ages, she's now more friend than aunt.

Whoever said a trouble shared is a trouble halved was right. As I sip my wine in front of the warm fire and tell Isobel about my meeting with Simon, I begin to feel better.

There's something so comforting about her. Maybe she's the mother figure I've been missing all these years.

'So,' she says, when I've told all. 'It's not looking good, is it? But we Flynns have always been fighters and survivors. How could we be anything else, with Jonas for an ancestor?

'You and I, Jessica, will fight this together and we will find a way to beat it.'

'Isobel, you're amazing. What would I do without you?'

It's true. Her strength is helping to keep me going.

'I cannot believe your father was so foolish. I'm sorry, Jessica,' she adds as I open my mouth to defend him, 'but how he could do something so irresponsible is quite beyond me.

'Did he think the problem with his eyesight would just go away if he didn't say anything to anyone? And to fail to inform the insurance company is nothing short of rank stupidity.'

I know she's right.

'Now,' Isobel continues, 'our first task should be to assess our current situation.'

We spend the next hour talking.

'If you ask me,' Isobel says, after we have tossed ideas around for some time, 'things are not as bad as they look at first sight.'

'How can you say that? I don't see how they can be much worse.'

'Think about it. What are the problems?'

'Money, or rather, lack of it. The insurance won't pay out unless Simon can perform a miracle.

'There are bills to pay, utilities, council tax, all those little luxuries of life we can't do without. We owe Max Corrigan

169

a whopping great sum to repay his investment, too.'

'So much for the problems. What about assets?'

'Just one. The house. Though it's more of a liability than an asset right now.'

'Don't be a pessimist, Jessica. As the only means you have of saving the Folly is the Folly itself, you need guests urgently. And you need to get the stables finished and start advertising the riding holidays.'

'Max thinks it's a potential goldmine,' I admit, thinking back to the day I'd shown him round.

'And so it is.'

'Aren't we forgetting one thing? I'm broke!'

'We'll come to that.' She stands up and collects the glasses. 'Much as I could fancy another of these, we need clear heads if we are going to crack this.'

As she heads for the kitchen she turns.

'By the way, I have a suggestion to make which might make a difference. But I'll just make a pot of tea first.'

I leap up and follow her.

'That's cruel! You can't leave me in suspense like that. What is it?'

Taking her time, she fills the kettle and switches it on.

'It's something I've been thinking about for a few days now. You may not agree to it, but I'm going to suggest it anyway.'

'I'm intrigued.'

'I've been thinking I'd like to move back here to live, and I wonder how you'd feel about me moving into the Lodge permanently.'

That's not what I'd expected. I've grown used to her company and I like the thought of having her close by, but I can't see how it will solve any problems.

'It would be wonderful,' I agree. 'But you hate it here! That's why you left.'

'That was when I lived in the house. It's quite different tucked away here in the cottage.'

'There will still be plenty of people around when we reopen,' I warn her.

'As I say, it will be different living here.

I'll be away from it all.'

'But, Isobel, apart from being able to talk things over with you — which will be wonderful — I don't see how it will help anything.'

The kettle boils and she makes the tea. We take it through to the sitting-room.

'Right,' she says when we are once more sitting by the fire. 'You need money, don't you? Well, I am offering to buy the Lodge.'

I'm astounded.

'You can't afford to do that!' I protest.

'I can. I'll sell my house in Devon.'

'I can't let you do that just to save the Folly. You love it in Devon.'

'Actually, I don't. The climate is better but, believe it or not, I miss this place. I miss the moor and the sea.

'When I left, I had no idea I'd miss it as much as I have. I allowed your grandmother's chaotic lifestyle to drive me away, and I realise now that was a mistake.

'I wish I'd thought of moving into this cottage then, instead of running away.'

I'm quite shocked to hear her talk like this.

'I'd no idea you regretted the move,' I told her. 'Why didn't you come home ages ago if you were so unhappy?'

'Stubbornness, I suppose. I wasn't going to let your grandmother know I'd made a bad decision. Then it seemed too late to change my mind.

'Anyway, I wasn't unhappy there, just unsettled. I realised some time ago I needed to come home, but it wasn't until I came back for Sam's funeral that it really hit me.'

'I don't know what to say, Isobel.'

'Say you agree. You'll be doing me a favour as well. It won't be one-sided.'

'How can I say no?'

'You can't. You'll be able to do the work on the house, set up your riding holidays and make enough to repay the loan.'

I go to my wonderful aunt and throw my arms round her shoulders in a huge hug.

'I can never thank you enough,' I tell

her, kissing her cheek.

'Nonsense. I should be thanking you for enabling me to come home. And you'll be able to tell that Max person to get lost.

'If that's what you really want, of course?'

As I walk back to the house later, I realise it's the last thing I want to do.

★ ★ ★

The next day I try calling Max again but he's still not answering his mobile, so I call his office. His secretary says he's busy with meetings and she'll tell him I called, but she can't say when he will be free.

I have to be satisfied with that.

Meanwhile, I have plenty to do in the house. Jim has finished painting the two rooms and I decide to go and clean so, next time Molly comes, we can move the furniture back.

I'm about to carry the vacuum cleaner up stairs when the phone rings.

It's Isobel.

I pick up the receiver.

'Isobel, good morning. Is everything all right?'

'Good morning, Jess. Yes, everything's fine. I wonder if you could give me a lift to the station tomorrow? I'm travelling back to see about putting my house on the market.'

'Of course, no problem. Will you be away long, do you think?'

'I hope not. I've spoken to my neighbour and she's going to keep an eye on it until it's sold.

'The estate agent thinks it will go quickly. Apparently it's the kind of property that appeals to people like me who want to retire there.

'All I need to do is find a removal firm and arrange for my furniture and belongings to be transported up here, which shouldn't take too long. Don't worry, I'll be back as soon as I can.'

'It will feel strange without you,' I tell her. 'I'll make sure the cottage is kept clean and aired for you while you are away.'

'Thank you, my dear. I'll check the train times and let you know when I need to leave. See you in the morning.'

'Forgive Me'

The next day is grey and overcast and it isn't long before the rain begins, the sort of rain I know will be set for the day.

I decide that, after I've taken Isobel for her train, I'll shut myself away in Dad's room and go through his desk.

By the time I get back from the station it's a typical Exmoor downpour, with water surging off the moor and running like a river down the combe.

Larkcombe Stream is rising fast and I make a mental note to check the pony field later to ensure the ground isn't flooding where the stream runs through it.

I change into dry clothes and go up to Dad's room. I still don't feel ready to go through his personal belongings, especially his clothes, but I must go through his desk.

Simon has been patient so far but I can't keep him waiting any longer.

I switch on the light and immediately

sense Dad's presence in the room. How long will it be, I wonder, before I feel he has truly gone.

Even with the curtains pulled back, the room is gloomy and outside all is dark, despite it being early morning.

There's usually an amazing view of the sea from this window but now sea and sky merge as one dark mass and it's impossible to see where one ends and the other begins.

I sit at the big, old oak desk. Three full-width drawers are topped by a bureau with a drop-down front which locks. If there's anything important here, that's where I'll find it, in the locked part.

Looking inside feels an invasion of his privacy, but it has to be done. I take the key from the pottery mug on the shelf where Dad always kept it and unlock the bureau.

I drop the front and scan the contents. Pigeonholes contain stationery, pens and pencils, postage stamps and odd letters kept for whatever reason.

There's correspondence from HMRC

which I flick through, but there's nothing unusual about it so I put it to one side to give to Simon. So far, everything looks normal and in order.

Between the pigeonholes, in the centre of the desk, is a small drawer. I open it and pull out a sheaf of papers which Dad has folded over so they'll fit into the drawer.

I unfold them and see they are from the opticians — the forms they issue after a consultation, containing results of the tests. The letters *AMD* leap out at me.

As I read, I begin to understand how Dad must have felt when he was given the diagnosis. To learn he'd likely lose his sight within the year must have been terrifying.

I put the papers with the others for Simon.

There's something else. I pull out another piece of paper and unfold it. What I see takes my breath away.

It's a letter addressed to me! The writing is shaky and almost illegible, but undoubtedly it is Dad's. I fight to control the sudden pounding in my chest.

Am I about to solve some of the mystery? I hardly dare look for fear of what I might find. With trepidation, I begin to read.

My darling Jess,

I don't know how to begin. I hope I will never have to send this letter and you will be home again before it becomes necessary and so I will be able to explain everything to you in person.

I'm afraid I've been very foolish but, believe me, everything I've done was done in an attempt to save you from worry.

I wanted you to be able to enjoy your travels and I was sure everything would be sorted by the time you came home.

That is still my hope. You've worked so hard over the years helping me with the Folly and you deserve to enjoy your break in peace.

However, in case I am unable to tell you face to face, I must explain why I have done what I have. You will eventually understand why I have to write this now, while I can.

Please try to forgive me.

Forgive you? I thought. Oh, Dad.

It started quite soon after you left. I thought it was just tiredness. I was having difficulty reading at first, then I found I was not seeing other things so clearly.

I thought maybe I needed glasses so I made an appointment with the optician for a check-up. The result was not good. It appears I have AMD.

They tell me it usually develops very slowly over years but the kind I have can develop very rapidly indeed. I have told Giles, as I thought someone near me should know, and he's helping me with some of the paperwork I'm having difficulty reading.

Soon I may not be able to see well enough to write at all, which is why I am setting all this down now while I can.

Anyway, to the point. Stupidly, I've allowed myself to be drawn into a deal which I now very much regret.

I saw it as a way of shortening the time it would take for us to complete our plans for the Folly, so we wouldn't have to worry too much if I lost my sight completely.

Giles wanted to see if I would be interested in a scheme he was involved with. He had been approached by a property developer who was looking for a suitable property in this area to develop into a hotel and conference centre.

He told me he and the developer thought the Folly would make an ideal site.

He was very persuasive and I saw it as a readymade business for us both. No more hard work with the B&B for you. No more struggling to make ends meet.

It would pay for the Folly to be fully renovated and put in order. Problems like the leaky roof would be dealt with.

I thought it could be the answer to everything. Giles seemed really keen so I agreed to join.

Then I found out we would have to give up ownership. I'd assumed we would still own the property, you see, and that the hotel company would pay us for the use of it. How naïve of me. It appears this man's intention was to gain complete ownership.

As soon as I realised what a terrible mistake I'd made, I said I was pulling out. What

I hadn't realised was that there was a termination clause in the agreement I'd signed which committed me to paying quite a large sum of money.

So I either stood to lose our house or I lost a great deal of money. As you will see, the house won.

What a fool I've been! At the very least, I should have had Simon look over the agreement but, quite wrongly, I was relying on Giles to be my eyes.

I thought if he was happy with the wording then it must be OK. After all, he was investing in it, too.

But why didn't he tell me about the get-out clause? I must tackle him about it.

Do you remember my old friend, Hugh Corrigan? Probably not. You were only a child last time he visited here.

I have been to see him to ask for his help. In the event of my losing my sight, you can trust him completely.

I am not telling anyone else as, after my dealings with Giles, I don't trust anyone else not to take advantage of my disability. I feel I must tell Simon, and I will do so, but first

I must talk to Giles.

I am going to drive to the harbour this afternoon to meet him, so I'll finish this letter later as there may be more news by then.

Whatever you think of me after reading this, my dear daughter, please remember that I love you.

And there the letter finishes. Dad clearly expected to write more after seeing Giles.

A thought occurs to me. Was that the day he crashed the car? The accident had taken place on the road to the harbour. Could this have been the same day?

In which case, had Dad been killed as a direct result of his dealings with Giles?

I feel anger build inside me. How could Giles have put Dad in such a position? How dare he! He'd known Dad was losing his sight and was relying on him for help.

Dad had trusted him, had always seen him as a friend, yet Giles had betrayed him when he was at his most vulnerable. Why?

I need to confront Giles about this. I

have to know the truth.

I replace the letter in the drawer, lock the desk and put the key back in the mug.

Then I change out of the tracksuit bottoms I'm wearing into clean jeans, grab my waterproof coat from the back door and go out. The rain is torrential and I'm soaked by the time I reach the car.

I don't think I have ever felt such rage, not helped by having to go out in this appalling weather. I know I probably shouldn't drive in this state but I'm beyond caring.

I start the engine and drive slowly down the drive, accustoming my eyes to the poor visibility. The wipers are on maximum, struggling to clear the water from the screen.

As I turn on to the narrow road to the harbour I hit a sheet of water which almost wrenches the steering-wheel from my hands and I struggle to retain control.

Water is pouring out of the hedge banks from the fields on either side, turning the road into a river. At any other time I would turn back but I've come this far and I'm determined to have it out with Giles.

I reach the coast but can barely see where the shingle beach ends and the sea begins. A thick grey mist of rain and cloud hangs over the road, covering everything in a ghostly shroud.

Luckily, I know the area well enough to find my way to the harbour front and park next to the sea wall.

I pull the hood of my coat over my head and climb out. The wind is even stronger down here and I struggle to close the car door before it's whipped out of my hands.

I battle across the road towards the Mermaid and push through the door into the reception lobby. There's no sign of Sally or anyone else but I'm in no mood to hang around waiting for someone to appear and, with my heart thumping, I stride down the corridor towards Giles's office.

His door is open and I can hear him

talking. His voice is raised and he is clearly having an argument.

Someone replies, and I freeze at the sound of the familiar voice. It's Max. What on earth is he doing here?

I keep quiet and listen, trying to make sense of the situation. I thought Max didn't even know Giles!

Parts of their conversation are loud enough for me to hear and, to my horror, I realise they are discussing — or more accurately, arguing about — Giles's involvement in the plan to make the Folly into a conference centre.

It confirms everything I've just read in Dad's letter.

'You were obviously happy enough to take advantage of the situation, Corrigan,' Giles is saying. 'It didn't take you long to weasel your way in there. The Folly will make a nice addition to your empire, eh?'

I don't catch Max's reply but I gasp as the meaning of Giles's remark sinks in. I've been completely wrong about Max. He's out to get ownership of the Folly, after all!

I must have made a sound because both men stop speaking and turn towards the open door, shock written across their faces.

I lash out at them in fury.

'How could you? How could you betray my father like that?'

My voice begins to break but with an effort I choke back the sobs. I will not break down in front of them.

'Dad thought you were his friend!' I shout at Giles. 'Some friend!'

'And you!' I turn to Max, not giving either man a chance to answer me. 'I thought you were my friend, but all this time you've been lying to me; pretending to help while you scheme to get your hands on the Folly.

'You're despicable, both of you!'

I rush out, heedless of the pouring rain, and run across to the car. I'm vaguely aware of one of them following me and calling but I can't hear above the noise of the wind. Anyway, I don't want to listen.

I slam the door, start the engine and throw it into gear. Uncaring, I turn the car and put my foot down. Part of me knows I'm driving recklessly but I'm so hyped up I have no thought for my safety. I just want to get home.

Is this how Dad felt when he came to see Giles? Was he so angry that he drove as madly as I'm doing now? If so, combined with his poor eyesight it's no wonder he crashed.

And it's not only Giles who's to blame. It's Max, too. The man I've come to trust. The man I've come to love.

The acknowledgement shocks me but I can't deny it. Yes, I love him.

I love the man who is responsible for my father's death. How ironic is that?

By now tears are pouring down my face and I can hardly see, but somehow I make it safely back through the village to the Folly. I drive up to the house and make a dash for the back door.

As I reach it, a car pulls up next to mine and I realise Max has followed me. He leaps out and comes after me, shouting.

'Jessica, wait! For heaven's sake, woman, will you stop and listen?'

I ignore him, run inside and slam the door before he can reach me. I don't want to listen to his excuses.

How can he possibly think I would want anything to do with him after this?

He bangs on the door.

'Jessica, let me in. We need to talk.'

'Go away!'

'Not until we've talked. Will you please let me in?'

'I don't want to talk to you ever again. Just go away and leave me alone.'

'Jessica, there are things you need to know. It's not what you think.'

'I know all I need to!' I shout. 'How could you do it? I trusted you. Dad trusted you, and you've betrayed us both.'

'I have no idea what you mean. For heaven's sake, open this door.'

'No! Just go away. Get lost.'

'I don't know what's got into you, Jessica, but as it's obviously not possible to have a sensible conversation with you,

I'll do as you wish and leave you alone.

'I have to go away for a few days to finalise a business deal so maybe I'll see you when I get back.'

I don't reply.

A moment later, I hear his car start up and accelerate down the drive.

I stand in the middle of the kitchen and let the tears pour down my face.

I've lost everything. Why did I have to fall in love with Max? He's been using me, as he'd used Dad.

His offers of help, the loan of the money, it's all a ploy to gain control of the Folly.

Giles tried to warn me about him and I didn't listen. But then, Giles betrayed Dad, as well.

I hate them both.

I take off my coat and boots and collapse on to a chair in front of the Aga. I can see from the clock it's way past lunchtime but I've never felt less like eating.

I've no energy to do anything so I curl up and sit staring into space, wondering how I'm going to cope with this second bereavement.

Because that's what it feels like. Like something inside me has died.

I wish Isobel were here. How I'd love to go to the Lodge and sit in front of her fire and open my heart to her. At least she is someone I can trust.

I must have fallen asleep because I wake with a start to find it's almost night. I drag myself to my feet and go upstairs.

I don't expect I shall sleep, even though I'm exhausted, but I shed my clothes, pull on pyjamas and go to the bathroom to wash my face and brush my teeth. I can't be bothered to do anything more.

I fall into bed and lie there, tossing and turning, for what seems like hours, listening to the rain drumming hard on the roof above my head like a hammer pounding my brain.

I've forgotten to check the buckets under the leak in the end attic room, another thing to worry about, but I can't face dragging myself out into the cold to go and look.

I'll face the consequences in the morning.

Keeping Busy

Amazingly, I do sleep, but wake the next morning with a dry mouth and a heavy head. Every time I move, my head protests as pain shoots through it.

I lie still and mull over the events of yesterday, trying to make sense of it all. It feels totally unreal, as if I've been to the cinema and watched a film. If I didn't feel so awful from the after effects of crying, I could almost believe I'd imagined it all.

I lift my head and groan. It's tempting to stay put but if I do I know my headache will only get worse. I need to get up and I need to have breakfast.

I can't remember when I last ate, but my stomach is telling me it was a long time ago.

I put on my dressing-gown and go to the bathroom. I'll have breakfast first and get dressed after I've eaten.

I look in the mirror and wish I hadn't. My face is blotchy from crying and my eyes are red-rimmed and puffy. It is definitely not a day to be seen.

Not that I need worry. I'm not expecting anyone in particular and the only person I really wouldn't want to see me looking like this is Max, and he isn't likely to call after yesterday.

Why would I care, anyway? We're finished. There's no future for us now.

I want so much not to believe Max is involved in the scheme to get the Folly, but I heard it with my own ears.

I think of the conversation I had with Giles when I told him about my plans for the stables. He said then that Max wasn't to be trusted, that he'd built his hotel empire by buying up businesses in trouble.

I didn't believe him, but obviously he was telling the truth.

What I find so hard to understand is how Max could deceive me as he had? Why did he let our relationship become so personal?

Why let me believe I meant something to him? Was he playing when he kissed me and made me fall in love with him?

Maybe I'm just another trophy, another victim of his power games. At least I found out in time, before our relationship went further. I must stop thinking about him.

My stomach rumbles and I go down to the kitchen and make myself a bowl of porridge. Comfort food.

I stir in a spoonful of honey and eat breakfast while I browse a magazine and try to lose myself in a short story, but it's impossible to concentrate. There's too much going on in my head.

I'm reading the first paragraph for the umpteenth time when I hear someone at the door. I immediately think of Max and begin to leap up.

Then I realise it will be Clare. I'd forgotten she was coming in today. I think of my appearance but again decide it doesn't matter.

'Morning!' she calls cheerfully as she comes into the kitchen. 'Mm, not such a good morning, I take it?' she adds with a frown on spotting me.

'What gives you that idea?'

'Oh, nothing much. Just the blotchy face and the red eyes.'

I grimace.

'That bad, eh? I hoped it might have improved by now.'

'I can see it's a good job I've come in today, though I almost didn't. The rain has stopped but it's still pretty nasty out there and there's plenty of water on the roads.

'But you obviously need a shoulder to cry on, so let me lose my coat and pour the caffeine and you can fill me in.'

She helps herself to the last cup of coffee.

'Shall I put another lot on?'

'Good idea. Thanks.'

She tops up the machine and carries her mug over to the table.

'Right,' she says, pulling up a chair, 'tell Auntie Clare all about it.'

Despite how I feel about Max and what he has done, I feel disloyal telling someone else about it.

'I don't know why I should feel this

way,' I say after I've told her the whole story.

'Because you're in love with him, of course.'

I stare at her.

'You knew?'

I'm amazed she noticed. I've only recently admitted it to myself.

'It's been obvious to everyone for ages; except to you, perhaps.'

'And to him,' I add bitterly. 'And now we know why, don't we? He's just been playing me along to get his hands on the Folly.'

Clare leans back in her chair and looks at me.

'Are you absolutely sure about that?' she asks. 'From what you've just said, that little bit of conversation you overheard could have meant anything.'

'I'm sure, all right. You should have seen their faces when they realised I'd heard them.'

'Jess, that doesn't mean anything. And I honestly can't see Max behaving like that.

'Mind you, I can see Giles doing something that underhand. I've always said there was something dishonest about him.'

'It looks as though you were right. But Dad had known him for years. How could he have been taken in?'

'Sometimes it takes a while for a person's true character to come out.'

'Like Max.'

'Oh, Jess.'

'It's made me determined to get this place back on its feet without Corrigan interference. Thanks to Isobel, it might not be too long before I'm in a position to repay the money Dad borrowed from Max.

'Then he won't have any hold on us at all and I can tell him to take a running jump!'

'I thought you told him to do that last night.'

'I did. Not that he'll take any notice until he gets his money back, I'm sure.'

'Well, for what it's worth, I think you should give him the benefit of the doubt until you've heard what he has to say. I don't think he's the kind of man who would do something so underhand.

'If he wanted the Folly he'd do it openly and honestly.'

'That's your opinion, is it?'

'It is.'

She drains her mug and takes it to the sink.

'The best cure for what you are suffering from is hard work, and there's plenty of that to do. So I suggest you finish that porridge, drink your coffee and go and have a shower and get dressed. You'll feel a lot better after that.'

She's right. I can't sit around all day feeling sorry for myself.

I leave her to wash the dishes and I head for the bathroom. After a hot shower, and wearing clean clothes, I feel up to tackling some work.

Somehow I have to get through the rest of the day and that means keeping busy.

Clare and I discuss new publicity and put together some adverts. She says she will revamp our website and Facebook page, which is good of her as, strictly speaking, all she is paid for is doing the books.

'What are friends for?' she says. 'Anyway, I enjoy it.'

'I am very grateful,' I tell her.

Time passes quickly once we are immersed in the planning.

Molly arrives after lunch, having walked up from the village.

'It's raining again. Like a blooming monsoon out there, it is,' she grumbles as she shakes off her wet coat in the porch. 'They're saying on the news it's going to last all week.

'Never mind. We should be used to it, shouldn't we?'

'I appreciate you making the effort to come up,' I tell her.

'If we stayed in every time it rained we'd never get anything done! And those rooms aren't going to clean themselves, so I'll go and make a start.'

'I'll come and help you,' I tell her.

A couple of hours later, we collect up

the cleaning stuff and admire the results of our labours.

'It's looking more like the Folly I remember,' I say. 'I reckon we are just about ready to go.'

'Does that mean you'll be opening for business again?' Molly asks.

'That's the plan. Clare is working on advertising so hopefully we'll get some bookings before long. Fingers crossed.'

'You should have a grand opening celebration,' Molly suggests. 'You could have a lovely party in the hall and use it to promote the business at the same time.'

'That's not a bad idea,' I reply.

The last thing I feel like at the moment is throwing a party but it would be a great way of letting people know we are open again.

I can invite people from the tourist information centres and holiday organisers and it might help to throw off the atmosphere of depression from the funeral and all the bad news I've had since.

'I expect that chap of yours will have lots of contacts you can approach.'

I scowl.

'I'm sure he will, but I don't think he'll be around much for a while.'

Molly looks at me.

'Like that, is it? Never mind, I expect it will all come out in the wash.'

I doubt it.

The rest of the day passes quickly. The house is ready.

Clare makes good progress with the advertising. She resurrects Dad's plans for the new leaflets and works on those and by the time she and Molly go home I really believe we have turned the corner.

We can be open for B&B in a matter of days and, thanks to Isobel, I'll soon be able to get the riding holidays up and running, which will bring in enough to start paying off Max. I hope.

I go to bed that night in an optimistic mood. As long as I don't allow myself to think about Max I'll be fine.

But it's easier said than done. The minute my head touches the pillow he's filling my thoughts.

I toss and turn, haunted by memories of the past days, remembering the barn dance and how he held me as we danced the Rozsa.

I can feel his presence as keenly as if he was here beside me: his arms round me holding me close; his warm breath on my cheek as he bends to kiss me and his lips on mine.

I shiver. How could I have been so easily taken in?

I think of our visit to see his father. I liked Hugh. He had been so open and friendly I can't believe there is anything underhand about him.

And if Hugh is honest, then why shouldn't his son be the same?

I have a flicker of doubt. Can Clare have been right when she said I might have misread the situation?

But I heard what I did. There's no doubt.

Eventually, I fall asleep, only to be haunted by dreams of Max; of riding on the moor with him and dancing in his arms under a moonlit sky.

Giles Confesses

I wake tired and unrefreshed but when I draw the curtains I'm relieved to see that at least it's no longer raining.

I shower and wash my hair and go downstairs, picking up the post from the front door as I go past.

The phone rings. Hoping it isn't more bad news, I answer and am relieved to hear Isobel's voice.

'Jessica? How are you?'

'Fine, thank you. I've missed you.'

'I've missed being there. I hope this isn't a bad time to call?'

'No, I'm just about to have breakfast.'

'This late?'

'Bad night, I'm afraid.'

'Not more bad news, I hope?'

It is tempting to tell her but it will take too long and, anyway, it's not something I want to talk about on the phone. Isobel is sure to hear it in my voice and I don't want her to worry about me.

'There's plenty to tell when you get

back,' I say. 'Clare and I are working hard getting ready to open again.'

'I'm glad to hear it.'

'How's the house business going?'

'Very well. The estate agent has been and it'll be on the market today. My neighbour has the keys and I've organised the removal firm.

'Everything is packed and waiting for the van to collect and, all being well, my belongings will arrive with you the day after tomorrow.

'That's my main reason for calling. Will you be free to collect me from the station later? There's a train that gets in around four o'clock, if you could manage that.'

'No problem. I'll see you at the gate.'

'Marvellous. Now I must go and get ready. See you soon.'

'Bye, Isobel.'

I disconnect, feeling more cheerful and looking forward to seeing her. I'll go to the Lodge later and check everything is in order for her return.

If I keep busy, hopefully I can stop my

mind dwelling on Max.

I'm about to go out when I hear a car pull up on the drive. I'm not expecting Molly today and, in any case, she usually walks up from the village and she has her own key, so I'm surprised to hear a knock at the door.

Puzzled, I open it and catch my breath in surprise.

'Giles!' I exclaim.

He's the last person I expected to see and it takes me a moment to gather my wits.

'How dare you come here after yesterday?'

I grab the door to shut it in his face but he puts out his hand and holds it open.

'Jessica. Please, let me talk to you.'

He leans against the door, preventing me from closing it.

'What earthly reason do you think I'd have for wanting to talk to you?'

He actually manages to look chastened. Or perhaps it's an act to wheedle his way in.

'No reason, I suppose. And I don't

blame you. But I would like the chance to explain. There are things you need to know.'

'I know all I need to!' I shoot back. 'What I overheard yesterday told me everything. Thanks to you and Max Corrigan, my father lost his life and I almost lost my home and my livelihood.'

'That's not how it was, Jessica. Please, if you will just let me explain?'

'Are you trying to tell me I misunderstood what I heard? That you aren't responsible for what happened to Dad? Because, if that's so, you must think I'm an idiot.'

He looks at me and sighs.

'What I'm trying to tell you, Jessica, is that it was my fault. I admit it. But Corrigan had nothing to do with it.

'I can't let you believe he was involved. I'm many things, but not that low.'

I can't believe I'm hearing this. Can it be true Max was not involved? Have I misjudged him, after all?

I want to believe it, and why would Giles say something like that if it wasn't true?

'I never meant it to happen the way it did,' he carries on. 'It seemed such a good deal at the time and I invested in the scheme myself.

'I wasn't trying to defraud Sam in any way. I lost money on it, too.'

'My heart bleeds for you.' I sniff.

'I'm not looking for sympathy. The thing is, I've worried for some time I could lose the Mermaid.

'Every storm or high tide the water comes closer and I know it won't be long before we are flooded out. You know what the coast is like there and how vulnerable the properties are.

'I thought the conference centre deal looked like a good backup plan. I hoped Sam and I would be partners in the Folly so, if I lost the Mermaid, I'd still have a business.'

I only half hear what he's saying. I'm still wondering if I was wrong about Max.

If I was, I've accused him unjustly and he will probably never forgive me for the way I spoke to him.

Giles is still talking.

'That's mainly what I wanted you to know. If you want to talk about it some-time, I'll tell you how it all happened.'

He turns to go, then pauses and looks back.

'I don't expect you to believe me, but I really am sorry, Jessica.'

Sorry? He's sorry? I shove the door hard against him and he stumbles back.

'Get lost, Giles! Just go away and leave me alone.'

I watch from the doorway as he climbs into his car and drives off. It's only after he's gone that the full meaning of his words sinks in.

Could this be why he had been so neg-ative about my plans for the Folly? Was he hoping I would fail so the Folly could be his?

Was it Giles, not Max, who was plan-ning a takeover?

Somewhere deep inside me a spark of hope flickers. Is there a chance Max might forgive me for the awful things I said?

It's urgent I contact him. I have to tell

him about Giles's visit.

I pull out my mobile to ring him but remember deleting his number last night in a fit of anger.

I pick up the landline and dial his office.

'I need to speak to Max Corrigan,' I say when the receptionist answers. 'I know he's away on business but do you have a number for him, please?'

She asks my name.

'Just a moment,' she says. 'I'll enquire for you.'

The line goes silent and I wait.

'I'm very sorry, Miss Flynn, but Mr Corrigan is still away from the office and not available to take calls at the moment.'

'You must have a contact number for him,' I plead.

'I'm afraid I have strict instructions he's not to be disturbed except in an emergency.'

'But this is an emergency! Please, I must speak to him.'

'I'm sorry, Miss Flynn. His instructions were quite clear.'

'Well, do you know when he will be back?'

'It depends how the meeting goes.'

I ring off. Clearly Max has left instructions he doesn't want to be contacted by me, and I can't blame him. It seems my only option is to wait until he comes back.

He'll have to contact me eventually because, as he is so fond of telling me, we have a business to run.

My phone pings and for a second my heart leaps, thinking it might be him, but it's only the alarm reminding me to collect Isobel.

It's so good to see her again. During the drive home from the station, I tell her everything that has happened.

'After what Giles said,' she comments, 'it's pretty clear Max wasn't involved in the deal. You need to give him a chance to explain what he was doing at the Mermaid.'

'I know, but I can't contact him. I think he's left instructions I'm not to be put through.'

'I can't believe he'd do that. If he's in meetings he'll have his phone switched off, won't he? And his secretary may have been told not to put anyone through; not you specifically. I think you're imagining things.'

She's probably right, but I can't stop thinking about the dreadful things I shouted at him, and the accusations I made. Will he ever forgive me?

Back home, Isobel seems really excited about living in the Lodge. I help her carry in her luggage and make sure she has everything she needs and we have a quick cup of tea together before I leave her to unpack.

Rescue

The weather is no better the next day, with heavy grey skies and a blustery, north-westerly wind.

I've seen this kind of weather often enough to know it could turn into something much worse as the day goes on, so I turn on the radio to hear the forecast.

Sure enough, amber weather warnings are in force for the whole of the south-west for gale-force winds and heavy rain.

There's no word from Max, but I don't really expect it. He knows where I am if he wants to contact me.

The weather grows steadily worse as the morning wears on. I go round the house making sure windows and doors are shut securely and putting buckets under the leaks in the attic. There's no sign of Clare and I doubt she will come in.

Mid morning, I phone Isobel to make sure she is all right.

'I'm fine,' she assures me. 'I've made

sure it's all secure and I have everything here I need. Don't worry about me.'

'Don't try to go outside, will you?' I warn her. 'It isn't safe in this wind.'

'You just look after yourself. Is the house holding up all right?'

'So far, so good. The buckets are all in place.'

'Batten down the hatches and I'll see you later when it's passed.'

I heat some soup for lunch while I can, in case we lose power. It wouldn't be the first time the power lines have blown into tree branches and shorted.

The rivers will be well up by now, rushing in torrents from the high moor and overflowing their banks as they tumble down the combes into the valley and the villages below.

I worry about the ponies. The Blackwater stream runs through their field and, although they are used to these conditions, if the water rises too high they won't be able to reach dry ground.

I stand at the window, wondering what to do. The drive already resembles a river as water pours down from the hill. I'll have to move them to the top field before it gets any worse.

In case Clare does arrive, I scribble a note to let her know where I'm going and prop it up on the table. Then I pull on waterproofs and wellies.

Just as I'm leaving, Clare rings.

'Sorry I haven't come in,' she says. 'There's no way I'm driving through this. It's getting pretty hairy out there.'

'I wouldn't want you to,' I assure her. 'It's far too dangerous. Stay put and I'll see you tomorrow.'

I drop my mobile into an inside pocket and go out. The wind takes hold and grabs the door out of my hands, throwing it back against the door jamb. I fight it back again and manage to close it.

I struggle to breathe as the wind snatches my breath away and I'm gasping as I battle my way down the drive and across to the ponies' field. Rain stings my face and forces its way inside my waterproofs, soaking the neck of the fleece I'm wearing underneath.

215

I'm cold and shivering before I've even reached the gate and I could kick myself for not doing this earlier.

My fingers are so numb with cold that manipulating the security lock on the gate is almost impossible. Rain running down my face obscures my view and I struggle to see to turn the dials, but at last it clicks and I open the gate.

The wind swings it back on its hinges, ripping it out of my grasp and raking my hand. I feel blood and I'm pretty sure I have splinters, but I can't afford to stop and think about it.

I go into the field and push the gate closed again. I call to the boys but the wind snatches the words away and I doubt even their acute hearing will pick up my voice.

The ground is already sodden. As I walk, my feet sink into the turf and water wells up round my boots. It's like walking through the marsh.

I squelch up the field, trying to locate the ponies, but it's impossible to see through the rain. I know they will have moved as high as they can, where the ground is slightly drier, so I move up the field and eventually, with relief, I see them in the farthest corner sheltering under a holly tree.

They whinny as they see me.

'Hello, boys,' I say. 'Rotten weather, isn't it? How about we get you out of here before it floods?'

They follow me up the field to the top gate that leads to higher pasture. They are not at all bothered by the weather. Their fellow ponies face far worse up on the exposed moor.

But at least, out there, they can keep moving to find high ground.

Again, I fight the lock on the gate, made more difficult as both ponies push against me, impatient to get into the lush grass of the ungrazed top field. Eventually, it gives and, fighting the wind, I open the gate, hanging on to it so it doesn't blow back on the ponies as they trot through.

I let the wind close it again and reset the padlock. They'll be safe there until the storm blows over.

Now all I have to do is fight my way back to the house.

The stream is rising rapidly. Like all Exmoor streams, the Blackwater rises alarmingly quickly in storm conditions. As I make my way back through the bottom field my feet sink further and further into the ground.

Water laps over the top of my boots and, to make it worse, it's now so dark I can no longer see properly.

I should have brought a torch. Again, I curse myself for not moving the ponies earlier in the day.

I reach in my pocket for my phone, hoping its torch might give me some light. I know the field well and, as long as I'm careful, I'll make it back safely. But the rushing water is powerful, pulling me off balance as it swirls round my legs.

Then something strikes me below the knee and, before I can avoid it, my feet are tangled in a long twiggy branch that must have broken off one of the trees.

I stumble and throw out my arms in an attempt to stay upright, but the drag of the water is too strong and I lose balance.

As I fall, my phone flies out of my hand into the water. My foot is completely wedged in the branch and I'm being dragged down.

As I hit the water my foot twists and I shriek with pain as I feel something in my ankle tear. A sick dizziness runs through me and I'm afraid I'm going to faint.

I shiver with cold and also with fear because I'm lying in a foot of water. Not deep, but enough to chill me to the bone if I don't get out of it fast. I'm fully aware of the dangers of hypothermia.

Gritting my teeth against the pain, I reach down and try to free my foot, but there's all kinds of vegetation wrapped round it, torn from the ground by the force of the water.

Desperately, I pull it away. The cold is helping to numb the pain in my ankle, but it's numbing the rest of my body as well.

I clear enough debris to be able to move my foot and, with a final effort, I twist free of the branch and pull myself clear.

I lie for a second, summoning strength, knowing I must move before I succumb to the cold. Gingerly, I stand up, testing the injured foot.

As pain shoots through me, I cry out. My head swims and I know I'm going to faint.

* * *

I've read that hypothermia has strange effects, like making you feel warm and comfortable when really you are on the verge of dying. This must be it, then, I decide; what it feels like to die.

I'm weightless, floating peacefully, encased in soft padded warmth, my head resting comfortably on a soft pillow.

Interesting. Dying is just like going to sleep; a rather pleasant sensation.

'Jessica.'

Somewhere on the edge of my cosy

cocoon I hear my name, but I push it away. It's disturbing my peace.

'Go away,' I mutter. 'I want to sleep.'

'Jessica!'

Now I'm being shaken.

'Wake up, woman.'

I drag my eyes open to see who is being so tiresome.

Max? What's he doing in my dream? I push him away and close my eyes again.

'Come on, Jessica, wake up.'

He's shaking me again. Slowly my head begins to clear and I realise it's no dream.

Max has his arms round me, holding me up, and the pillow I've been dreaming about is his chest.

Why is he here? Am I imagining it?

'Talk to me, Jessica.'

I'm not imagining it. He really is here! My heart gives a leap.

'What happened?'

'That's what I would like to know, but first we need to get you inside. Can you walk?'

I shake my head.

'I caught my foot and twisted my ankle or something.'

It's coming back to me now and I can remember what happened.

'I must have fainted.'

'Right, there's only one thing for it. Put your arm round my neck.'

Before I can protest, he's scooped me up in his arms and is carrying me through the storm, out of the field and back to the house.

Battling against the wind as he opens the back door, he carries me into the kitchen and sets me down next to the table.

'Hang on to that while I get you out of these waterproofs.' He strips off my wet outer layer, then removes his own and drops them all in the sink.

Then he picks me up again and carries me into the sitting-room where the fire I lit earlier is still clinging to life.

He drops me on the sofa and turns to stoke the glowing embers and pile on some more logs.

'What on earth were you doing going

out in this weather?' He sounds cross. Does that mean he still cares?

'I had to move the ponies,' I explain.

'I've never heard anything so stupid as going out there on your own in these conditions! Why leave it so late?'

'Because I didn't think about it earlier,' I retort. 'I had my mobile with me.'

I don't mention I dropped it.

'A fat lot of use that would have been if you knocked yourself out. Which you did!'

'I don't know what you're getting so het up about.'

'Don't you? Then you have even less sense than I thought!'

'Don't shout at me!'

Shock is kicking in as I realise what a close call I've had. If Max hadn't found me . . .

We glare at each other. Then, to my surprise, he begins to unzip my fleece.

I grab hold of it.

'What do you think you are doing?'

'Getting you out of these wet clothes. Or do you want to get pneumonia?'

'I'm quite capable of taking them off myself, thank you.'

'Fine.' He shrugs. 'Tell me where I can find a blanket.'

'In the linen cupboard at the top of the stairs.'

He leaves the room and I wonder what to do next. I'm certainly not taking anything off till I have something to wrap round me.

The warmth of the fire is comforting and I'm feeling a little better, more relaxed, even though my ankle is killing me.

Max comes back with a blanket.

'Here,' he orders. 'Now, get out of those wet clothes and give them to me.'

'When you've left the room.'

He folds his arms and looks at me.

'I think I should stay, don't you? You might find it difficult with that ankle.'

'You are joking!' I exclaim. 'I can manage perfectly well, thank you.'

Determined to show I can do it without him I sit up, but as I swing my legs round into a sitting position pain shoots through me and I sway.

'You were saying?'

Heavens, the man's infuriating.

'Well, at least turn your back.'

He grins and that little scar next to his eye crinkles. I haven't noticed it for a while but it suddenly seems very sexy indeed.

Our eyes lock and his expression changes and softens. Desire surges through me and I see the same desire reflected in his face.

I hold my breath as he moves closer and sits beside me on the sofa. He places his hands either side of me and slowly leans forward until our lips are almost touching.

I can feel his breath as he draws closer and my own breathing pauses in anticipation.

As his lips finally touch mine, I close my eyes and allow myself to drown in his kiss.

I'm aware of him gently removing my fleece. I keep my eyes closed. I want to revel in the moment, to enjoy the sensation of his face against mine.

Then, unthinking, I stretch my leg and cry out as a bolt of pain shoots through me.

The spell is broken and Max sits up.

'You'd better remove the rest yourself,' he says, his voice gruff with emotion.

I swallow and nod. Without being asked, he turns and leaves the room.

As I finish undressing and wrap myself in the blanket, I think over the extraordinary events of the afternoon.

Our relationship, if that's what it is, has undergone a subtle change. I can no longer doubt that I love Max.

What I'm not so sure of is whether or not he loves me.

The fire is burning brightly now and the room is warm but I'm determined to keep the blanket safely in place.

Max comes back carrying a tray.

'I thought you might like a hot drink,' he says, putting a mug down on the table next to me. 'I hope you like hot chocolate?'

'I love it. Thank you.'

'These might help, too.' He hands me

some painkillers.

He sits beside me. Cautiously, I extend an arm to pick up the mug. The blanket begins to slip from my shoulder and I grab it quickly.

'Here, let me.' Max tucks the blanket more securely round me and smiles. 'You can trust me, you know.'

'I know,' I reply. And I realise it's true. I do trust him. 'Then relax and enjoy your drink. I won't leap on you at the first sign of bare flesh.' His mouth curves in a wicked grin. 'Not that I don't find the prospect tempting.'

The feeling is mutual and I know I'm flushing. Hopefully, he'll think it the heat of the fire.

I concentrate on drinking the chocolate and eventually my pulse slows. 'Better?' he asks when I've finished. I nod. 'Much. Thank you.' 'How's the ankle?' 'Murder, but the pills are helping.' 'Good.' He puts his arm round me.

'We'll see how it is in the morning and I can run you to A&E if necessary.'

Max and Giles

What with the hot drink and the fire, and the comfort of being in Max's arms, I'm feeling relaxed and sleepy. I lean into him.

Who'd have thought we'd be sitting here like this after the way we parted?

'Max,' I murmur, 'why did you come here today?'

'My secretary told me you'd been trying to get in touch.'

'I wanted to phone you but she wouldn't give me your number. I thought you didn't want to speak to me.'

'She was just following orders not to give out the number to anyone.'

'I was convinced you were deliberately shutting me out.' I tilt my head up. 'Not that I'd have blamed you, after the way I yelled at you.'

'I wasn't shutting you out. I was just very busy. Anyway, she said it sounded urgent so I decided to come and see what the problem was.'

'You could have phoned.'

'I did. There was no reply. Which might have something to do with your madcap venture to get yourself drowned.'

'Oh.' I blush.

'So I drove over instead. And it's a good job I did. I saw the note you left for Clare. The one sensible thing you did today.'

Thank goodness I hadn't binned that note after Clare rang to say she wasn't coming.

'Well, I'm glad you found me. I might have been in trouble if you hadn't turned up when you did.'

'That, I think, is an understatement.'

I let my head rest against Max's shoulder as he pulls me into him and tilts his head towards mine. We sit listening to the logs crackling in the grate. I feel happy.

One thing still bothers me. I'm reluctant to mention it for fear of destroying this new harmony, but if I don't settle it in my mind it will be between us for ever.

Assuming we have a 'for ever'.

'Max, if I ask you something, will you

promise not to take it the wrong way?'

'As I don't know what you want to ask, I can't say how I'll take it, but I'll try.'

'I don't think I'll be able to rest if I don't get to the bottom of it.'

I feel him move slightly further away and I sense a distance between us.

'You want to know about that conversation with Giles.'

'Yes. I know I was wrong about you, but I need you to explain. Please?'

'Why did you decide you were wrong?'

'Giles came to see me. He must have had an attack of conscience, because he said he couldn't let me go on thinking you were involved in the deal.'

'He wanted to tell me about it but I told him to go away.'

'That's getting to be a habit of yours.'

'I know. But I still don't know why you were there that day.'

'First, you can tell me why you were there. On a day like that you shouldn't have been driving. That road was treacherous.'

Max doesn't know about Dad's letter.

'I was sorting Dad's desk,' I tell him, 'looking for papers for Simon, and I found a letter Dad started to write to me. It explains a lot of what's been going on.'

I sit up.

'Why don't you read the letter? It'll be easier. It's in the centre drawer of his desk in his bedroom. You'll find the key in the pot on the shelf.'

While I wait for him to fetch the letter, I think how my life has changed since I returned to England. I sense it is about to change again.

Max returns with the letter and sits beside me to read it. As he reads, I watch his face become more and more angry.

'You thought I was the property developer they were involved with?'

'No, not then. But I was so angry with Giles I didn't stop to think. All I knew was I had to see him, to tackle him about what he'd put Dad through.

'When I got there and heard you both talking in his office, discussing hotel chains and the Folly . . .' I shrug. 'I suppose I jumped to conclusions and just assumed you were the developer involved.'

'I can see how you might have thought that, and I can certainly understand why you were angry enough to assume the worst. But I hope you are now truly convinced I had nothing to do with it?'

'Of course I am. I think, even if Giles hadn't told me, I'd have realised — as soon as I calmed down enough to think straight – that you would never have done anything like that.'

He takes my hand and holds it.

'Good. I'm glad.'

'But I still don't know why you were there.'

'I'd been looking into Giles's background. After what you told me about his comments about me, and his reaction to your plans, I began to get suspicious that he had designs on the Folly himself.

'I didn't say anything in case I was wrong and I wanted to be sure of my facts first. 'I found out about the deal he was trying to fix, which ties in with what Sam wrote in this letter, and went to see him, hoping I could persuade him to reimburse some of the money Sam lost.

'That's why you overheard us discussing the deal.'

'I am so sorry for doubting you.'

'Well, I can't promise he'll come up with the goods, though he did agree he owes you something. Unless we take him to court there's nothing we can do to force him to pay up.'

'I can't do that. It would bring Dad into it and I'd rather do without the money than drag his name through the courts and newspapers.'

'I guessed you'd say that. Now, if that answers your question, it's time you were in bed. I don't feel like driving over the moor at night in this weather so, unless you have any objection, I shall stay here.'

My pulse jumps again at the thought of him sleeping in the same house.

'Lucky you have all these spare rooms, isn't it?' he adds, grinning.

I swear he enjoys winding me up.

'OK, let's get you upstairs.'

I grab the edges of the blanket as he

scoops me up in his arms again and carries me upstairs to the first floor. He looks at the stairs leading up to the attics and groans.

'Did you really have to have your bedroom right at the top of the house?'

'Not up to it?' I tease.

'I should watch it, if you don't want to be dropped from a great height!' He makes it up the stairs to my room and places me gently on the bed.

'Can you manage now?'

'I'll be fine. And I've just remembered there are some crutches somewhere in the cupboard on the landing.'

'I'll look.'

He disappears and returns with the crutches.

'Useful to have around,' he comments. 'They're a souvenir from when Freddy threw me some years back. I've had plenty of practice with them.'

'Please take care. I assume I'll find bedding in the linen cupboard?'

'Yes. Help yourself.'

'Thank you. I shall go and find myself

a room and I'll see you in the morning.'
He bends and kisses my forehead.

'Goodnight, my love.'

It's only after he's gone downstairs that the significance of his words hit me.

A Different Partnership

I discover the next morning that I have a throbbing ankle and I'm aching all over.

With the help of the crutches I hobble to the bathroom and wash and dress. Then, leaning on a crutch on one side and hanging on to the banister rail with the other hand, I manage to make it down to the kitchen.

Max is at the table, drinking coffee and listening to the news. He's clearly fresh from the shower and his hair is damp and curling where it touches the nape of his neck.

I imagine sliding my finger into one of those curls and watching it spring back as it's released. Remembering his kiss last night, I begin to feel the nerves in my own neck tingle.

He looks up and smiles.

'Good morning. You look as though you slept well.'

'I did. Thank you.'

'How's the ankle?'

'It could be worse. I don't think there is any need to go to the hospital, thank goodness.'

I hobble to a chair and sit down.

'Could you pass me a coffee, please, though? I don't think I can manage without spilling it.'

He fills a mug and puts it on the table in front of me. As he does so, he bends down and drops a kiss on my forehead.

What is it about my forehead? What I really want is for him to kiss me properly.

Max must have read my mind because the next thing I know his lips are on mine and they aren't in any hurry to leave.

At that moment, the back door flies open and we both look up.

Isobel is standing in the doorway with her mouth open.

'Oh!' she manages.

I can't help laughing. I've never known my aunt lost for words before.

'Isobel, come on in.' I indicate Max. 'This is Max. Max, meet my great-aunt Isobel.'

He goes over to her, holding out his

hand.

'I'm very pleased to meet you. May I get you something to drink? I'm afraid Jessica is slightly incapacitated this morning.'

She notices the crutch.

'What have you done?' she asks me. 'What's going on?'

She turns to Max.

'No, I don't want anything, thank you. Except an explanation.'

I smile at her.

'It's a long story, Isobel. Come and sit down and let us fill you in.'

* * *

Once Isobel has gone back to the Lodge, shaking her head and looking bewildered, I ask Max to pass me the phone.

'I need to ask Emma to make sure the ponies are OK after yesterday.'

'I can do that.'

'I assumed you'd want to get away. You must have work to do.'

'I phoned my secretary earlier. She'll

cope with anything that needs doing for a while.

'I'm not leaving you on your own until I know you can move around safely.'

A warm glow surges through me at the realisation he does care about me.

'Thank you. In that case, if you could make sure the fences are sound and the boys are safe, I'd be very grateful.'

'No problem.'

He's been gone a few moments when the landline phone rings. Simon's name comes up on the display and I feel a flash of alarm, wondering what bad news he has for me now.

I sit on the settle in front of the Aga and brace myself to hear the worst.

'Simon, hello.'

'Jessica.'

He sounds cheerful so maybe this isn't bad news.

'I'm pleased to say that we're making progress. Probate is through so we can move ahead at last.'

I breathe a sigh of relief.

'Thank goodness. I was beginning to

think we'd never get there.'

'That's not all. I had a visit from Giles Mason this morning.'

Why would Giles go to see Simon?

'What did he want?'

'Believe it or not, he came to pay you some money. He said he owed it to Sam and you would understand what it was for. Does that make any sense to you?'

I can hardly believe it.

'Yes, it makes perfect sense. Can I ask how much?'

Simon names a figure and I realise Giles must have repaid a large part of the default payment Dad had to find.

I'm lost for words.

'Jessica? Are you all right?'

'Oh, very much all right.'

'Perhaps you'll enlighten me as to what it's all about?'

'It's a long story.'

'Well, I need your signature on some papers so you can fill me in when you come to sign them.'

'Is there any chance you could come here? Only I'm on crutches.'

'Crutches?'

'Another long story, I'm afraid.'

'My goodness, I'm intrigued. OK, I'll try to get over later today. Something tells me I should allow plenty of time.'

He rings off and I sit holding the phone, wondering if I'm dreaming. I can't wait to tell Max when he comes in.

I'm just beginning to realise the implications of all this. With the money from the sale of the Lodge, and the payment from Giles, I can go ahead with my plans for the stables and bringing the Folly back to life.

I jump as Max comes through the door kicking off his mud-caked boots.

'The ponies are fine,' he tells me, 'but I'm glad I won't be the one who has to groom them.'

'Max, I've just had the most incredible news. Simon just called to say Giles went to see him!'

I recount Simon's message.

'Isn't it wonderful?'

'So he came up with the goods, after all.'

Max sits down beside me, resting his

arm along the back of the settle, his hand on my shoulder.

'Thanks to you,' I reply. 'It must have been because of what you said to him that day at the Mermaid. With that, plus the money from the sale of the Lodge . . .'

I realise he doesn't know about Isobel buying the Lodge and quickly explain.

'So there's nothing to stop me going ahead with everything now. I can do all the work we planned on the stables and the Folly.'

'I'm very pleased for you.'

'I can even repay most of your loan.'

He stretches his legs out towards the Aga and I wait for him to say something.

After a long silence, he turns towards me.

'You realise,' he says, 'this could mean the end of our partnership?'

My heart sinks.

'I don't understand.'

'You'll no longer need me. You'll have everything you need to run your business without me; which is what you wanted.'

It might have been, once, but now I

can't bear the thought of Max no longer being around.

'But . . .' I start to say.

He interrupts.

'However, perhaps I could suggest a different kind of partnership.'

My heart leaps. Does he mean what I think he does?

'Would you care to clarify that?'

'I'd be delighted. Something a little more like this.'

He tilts my head towards his and our lips meet.

'I think,' I tell him eventually, 'you can take that as a yes.'

We do hope that you have enjoyed reading this large print book.

Did you know that all of our titles are available for purchase?

We publish a wide range of high quality large print books including:
Romances, Mysteries, Classics
General Fiction
Non Fiction and Westerns

Special interest titles available in large print are:
The Little Oxford Dictionary
Music Book, Song Book
Hymn Book, Service Book

Also available from us courtesy of Oxford University Press:
Young Readers' Dictionary
(large print edition)
Young Readers' Thesaurus
(large print edition)

For further information or a free brochure, please contact us at:
Ulverscroft Large Print Books Ltd.,
The Green, Bradgate Road, Anstey,
Leicester, LE7 7FU, England.
Tel: (00 44) **0116 236 4325**
Fax: (00 44) **0116 234 0205**

Other titles in the
Linford Romance Library:

THE THIRD SON

Philippa Carey

Lord Peter has disgraced the family once too often. Now his father is giving him one last chance to redeem himself. Go to the Devon estate and find out what is wrong with it: solve the problems, and the estate is his. Fail, and he will be cast off to make his own way in the world. Once in Devon, Lord Peter discovers resentful tenants, a thief, vicious smugglers — and, most significantly, a beautiful blind girl and her very clever dog . . .